WILLIS WILBUR

Meets His Match

by Lindsey Leavitt

iLLustrated by Daniel Duncan

PENGUIN WORKSHOP

To the Alliterati + all my UCFA family

W

PENGUIN WORKSHOP
An imprint of Penguin Random House LLC, New York

First published in the United States of America by Penguin Workshop,
an imprint of Penguin Random House LLC, New York, 2022

Text copyright © 2022 by Lindsey Leavitt, LLC
Illustrations copyright © 2022 by Daniel Duncan

Visit us online at penguinrandomhouse.com.

Library of Congress Cataloging-in-Publication Data is available.

Printed in the United States of America

ISBN 9780593224076

1st Printing

LSCC

Design by Julia Rosenfeld

CHAPTER 1

My Networking Opportunity!

The only time more hectic than the first days of summer are the *last* days of summer. One glance at my summer bucket list reminded me I had not completed every single memorable adventure I'd set out to do before I became a fourth grader! There were only a few more days left before school started, and I still had to . . .

1. Open an office for my brand-new life coaching business in the strip mall next to Michael Morales's real estate company. Possibly share a sign together.

2. Taste test five or six fancy cheeses so I can be

interesting at future adult parties.

3. Network at a party.

4. Climb Mount Everest.

    a. Research tall mountains in Colorado I can climb since Mount Everest is sorta far.

    b. Find someone to hike a mountain with me who really likes carrying a backpack because there is no way I can fit all my stuff into one bag, and actually the altitude would make it really hard to breathe, so it's probably best if I don't carry a bag at all.

        i. Buy a new backpack just in case.

        ii. Maybe just walk up a rolling hill instead of a mountain?

There were fifteen other items on the list, but I'd already done those, and I shouldn't talk too long about my success because I'd have to talk for three days straight. Even though I couldn't finish the whole list, I would have an opportunity to accomplish number three. Party networking.

And wow, I was dreading it.

"Willis, you know I love business attire," Margo said. Margo was my life coaching client. A life coach is someone who helps people make goals and progress in their life. She was also sorta my friend. We were in my living room, waiting for my dad to come home and give us a ride to Greysen Robison's end-of-summer party. "But wearing a blazer and bow tie to a swimming party is maybe too . . . professional," she finished.

PRO TIP #1:
There's no such thing as
dressing too professionally.

I looked down at my outfit. The blazer was a hand-me-down from my cousin, who wore the seersucker jacket at a wedding. In case you don't know, seersucker is a striped and puckered fabric that screams summer. *Screams* it. "I'm not going swimming. I'm going fishing. For clients. Get it?"

Margo shook her head. "Didn't you just spend the entire summer educating me on the value of kid activities? And now you're dressing like . . . my grandpa at a horse race."

It was probably a good thing I didn't show her the fedora.

Dressing up helped me feel more confident. And I needed that feeling, especially at a pool party, which I didn't usually love. Also, I needed to look nice for my potential new clients. I started my life coaching business in June because I wanted to win the scholarship offered by Business Owners Organization, or BOO. Back then, I only had two clients—Margo and a guinea pig named Dog. I didn't end up winning the scholarship, but I did grow the business in my garage office all summer. Now I had eleven life coaching clients, but there was still opportunity to level up. I needed to hire more life coaches and branch out into other states and record a podcast and start a 401(k), whatever that was.

My sister, Logan, walked into the living room wearing a lab coat. It was a million degrees outside, and she was only wearing a coat because she wanted to look important at STEM camp. Which is very different from wearing a seersucker suit at a pool party.

"Dad's dropping me off first. I can't be late."

"I know," I said.

"I need to get a good seat at the awards ceremony because I won so many things."

"I know," I said.

"I did the spreadsheet for next week's schedule." She smoothed out her lab coat. "Margo showed me how to do it."

"I know," I said.

Logan frowned at me. "Why are you wearing that jacket? You look like you work at an old-timey candy store."

"Exactly!" Margo said.

"I'm getting in the car," I said.

On the drive, Margo and Logan chatted with Dad about Logan's summer success. She started off at day camp part-time while being my sorta business manager for life coaching. One week, day camp had this science theme, and Logan did so great that Mom switched her over to a STEM camp, and she never looked back. Logan was still helping me expand my business, but she didn't seem as excited about it anymore.

Not that I had time to worry about my sister right now. After we dropped her off, I shifted all my focus to the big thing ahead. The party. I stared out the window and repeated positive affirmations in my head.

I will be confident and friendly.

I will find clients who need my services.

I will use my many months of experience to build my business.

I will dazzle and delight.

I will become a billionaire before I turn sixteen.

"You ready, Willis?" Margo asked.

Dad pulled up to the house. A kid in a flamingo inner tube walked past our car.

Ready or not, the party was starting.

CHAPTER 2

The Big Summer Splash!

Someday I will go to six parties all in one day, like they do at the Oscars. There's the before-the-Oscars party, then the red carpet, then the Oscars, then the after-the-Oscars party, then the after-after-party, and then . . . a lot of people don't know about this one . . . there's also an after-after-*after*-party. I'll have to go to all of these parties to congratulate my celebrity clients on realizing their dreams. It comes with the life coaching territory.

But today I was just at one party, and that one was extra overwhelming. First, there were the kids inside the

house, who were running around blasting each other with NERF guns and shouting "Zombie War!" I didn't see how sticks of foam with little suction things on the end had anything to do with battling undead creatures, but imagination games weren't always my thing.

I skirted around the NERF kids and into the kitchen. There was a veggie platter and fruit salad, but no one seemed to be eating it. Next to that were a few pizza boxes filled with leftover crusts. A boy I'd never seen before was nibbling on a piece of broccoli.

He smiled at me. "Hey! Sweet party, right?"

"What? Oh yeah. Totally." I grabbed a few baby carrots. I'd taken sizeable kid inventory of every neighborhood within ten miles of me, not to mention gone through the yearbook of three elementary schools and two middle schools. I had charts and diagrams of interests and activities so I could be prepared to meet prospective clients.

I stared at his long, floppy hair and wrist full of bracelets. Nothing came to me. "Do I know you?"

"Probably not, I'm new. Colt." He gave me a friendly nod. "Just moved here from the Bay Area."

"What bay?"

"Ha. That's funny."

I wasn't trying to be funny, but sometimes it happened by accident. "Thanks."

10

"Yeah, Colorado is something else. Being inland is weird, but I'm digging the Rockies."

"Sure." In case you couldn't tell, I was not the best at small talk. I much preferred big talk. But once I warmed up a bit, I was really good at chatting up prospective clients. "I like your bracelets."

He held up his wrist. "Helps align my chakras. I can get you one if you're interested."

Adrian James poked his head into the kitchen but froze when he saw me. "Oh hey, Willis. Any pizza left?"

I shrugged very casually. "Nah."

"Okay." He zipped back outside. This was about as much as I talked to Adrian in public because we had a shared secret. I'll tell you more about that later, but for now I had to act cool.

"Anyway, Colt. Tell me more about this bay."

"That kid that just left? He's strong purple," Colt mused. "Intuitive but keeps secrets."

11

Adrian was not wearing any purple, and Colt did not know him at all, so it was a weird conversation starter. He tilted his head to the side. "And you are . . . beige. That's cool. Practical. With a little bit of orange energy."

My natural instinct as a life coach was to guide someone into a better version of themselves. And in Colt's case, a less-weird version. Calling someone a color is very kindergarten (and also, I'm clearly azure if I'm any color at all).

"Colt, I don't know what bay people do, but here we use names instead of colors. I'm Willis Wilbur, neighborhood life coach." I handed him my card. Wow, did he need it. It was a good thing he met me so soon after moving here.

Colt held my card up in the light and smiled. "Life coaching, eh? How'd you get started in that?"

Obviously, that was a very long story I couldn't get into with Colt right there in the kitchen. But basically it started when my best friend, Shelley, went to Hawaii for the summer. (She was coming back tonight!) Shelley and I were supposed to go to band camp, but then she left, so I suddenly had to find a summer activity so my mom wouldn't make me do something horrible like baseball poetry camp. So I found life coaching. I really liked working with others and helping them make positive changes.

See? That's the long answer. Instead, I just said, "Everything fell into place. I have a great reputation, and I really love my job. As Michelle Obama once said,

'Success isn't about how much money you make; it's about the difference you make in people's lives.'"

"Cool. Rock on."

Now that I'd introduced myself, gotten to know Colt, and told him about my job, it was time to help him see why he could use my services.

PRO TIP #2:
Know yourself so you can sell yourself.

"You know, I could help you work through your issue of calling people a color instead of a name."

"I was just reading your aura, Will." He laughed. "Aura reading is actually one of the talents I use in my job. Anyway, rad to meet ya. Snazzy blazer, by the way."

And then Colt walked outside like calling someone the color beige was a totally nice and normal thing to do. BEIGE? Me?

Clearly he was new here. Clearly he had a strange job if reading colors was part of it. Clearly my blazer suddenly was way too hot and not snazzy, so I shrugged it off and followed Colt outside to ask what an aura was, anyway. And also to tell him to switch it to blue *pronto*.

You're not going to guess what happened next. Okay, maybe you can. Let's just say, it was a good thing I took the blazer off because . . .

As soon as I was outside, someone cannonballed into the pool and I got splashed BIG TIME!

Even my bow tie got wet.

"Whoa!" Spencer Limbaco called. "Sorry, Willis!"

Margo ran over with a towel. "I'm not going to say I told you so, but . . ."

I took the towel. This party was not turning out as well as I had hoped. "It's fine. I'm fine."

"At least Spencer said sorry," Margo said.

"That's because I worked with him and Ella. Couples coaching." I shook out my hair. Technically, I wasn't supposed to discuss information on my clients, but I figured here it was fine since everyone knew Ella and Spencer used to bully me. He wasn't trying to splash me on purpose. That's progress.

I realized I should bring up this small victory—an apology for splashing—in our next session. I reached into my pocket to write that down, but my pocket with my notebook was all wet. So were my business cards.

"Great. Awesome. Wonderful. Terrific!" I yelled.

"Willis . . ."

16

I hugged the towel closer to me and took a seat in the shade. Excessive sarcasm? I really had to get control of myself.

I breathed in deep. Drank some water. Ate fruit salad. Envisioned my bright, colorful (not beige!) future. Then I laid out my business cards in the sun.

My phone was in my dry pocket. I used this to call my best friend, Shelley.

"Willis? Aren't you at the party?" she asked.

"Yeah, I'm just making sure you checked in for your flight."

She laughed. "I'm at the gate right now, waiting to board."

Then there was a pause, which I was going to fill in with all my frustration and maybe insecurity, but Shelley already knew me so well that I didn't have to.

"Don't worry," she said. "We'll be together again soon! Go have fun, okay?"

"Make sure you packed earplugs for your flight!" I hung up.

I couldn't let the weirdness I felt from that new kid calling me beige get in the way of my own visions and dreams. This party was actually pretty fun, for a pool party. And I still looked professional enough with my bow tie. So I stood up, squared my shoulders, and introduced myself to three new kids. (Well, I was new to them. Remember, I'd memorized almost everyone around me, which is part of pre-networking.)

Everything was fine. Because tonight:

1. I got to see Shelley!

2. I found out my new teacher.

18

CHAPTER 3

My Best Friend
Is Back!

MY BEST FRIEND WAS BACK! MY BEST FRIEND
WAS BACK!

I ate two pieces of cake at the party so I was *extra*
excited to see Shelley again. As you know, I'd waited to
see Shelley all summer after she went to Hawaii with her
family instead of going to band camp with me, which
ended up being a great arrangement because . . .

1. I can't actually play an instrument.

2. I formed a life coaching *empire,*

    a. which led me to more friends

b. and discovering my destiny.

3. And also Shelley came out of her shell while she was in Hawaii, which you might not get because it's kind of an inside joke and no one knows Shelley as well as I do, not even Margo, no matter what she says.

I stood on Shelley's driveway with a glittery "Welcome Home!!" poster, dancing in place because I was so excited and maybe because I also drank two cans of Sprite in addition to eating the cake. Every car that whisked by made me bouncier. The Kalani family got a rideshare from the airport, so I had no idea which car would pull into the drive. A minivan slowed down, but they were dropping off someone two doors over. Then a sedan pulled in. It was stopping! I steadied the sign, but . . .

It was Margo. Holding a whole bunch of balloons and a sign even bigger than mine.

"Looks like we had the same idea." She looked at my sign, then down at her own. "I mean, I had it bigger. But still."

Even though Margo and I spent so much time together this summer, we hadn't discussed this moment—the day that our best friend came home. Or how things would be when Shelley got back, both with Shelley and with each other.

But we didn't need to worry about it. We understood each other. We even liked each other now. So Margo handed me a few balloons, and we did a Shelley-is-almost-home dance together.

And then another car pulled up, and this time it *was* the Kalani family, and Margo and I jumped up and down. Shelley ran up and gave both of us a hug in a bouncy, three-person circle. It was awesome.

"Let's go inside so I can give you souvenirs!" Shelley said.

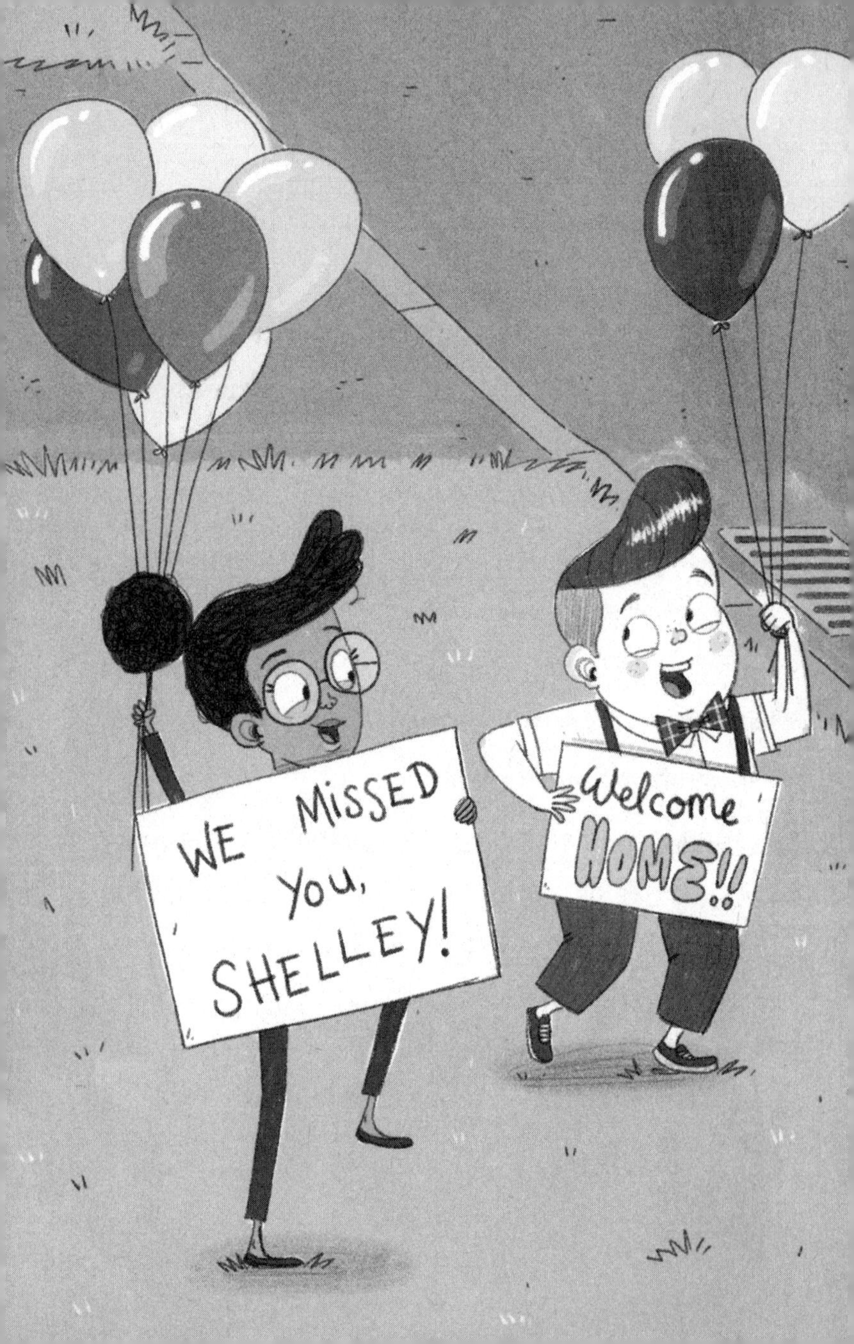
WE MISSED YOU, SHELLEY!
Welcome HOME!!

We scrambled up to Shelley's room, which was very clean because she hadn't been home messing it up for over two months. She dropped her suitcase on the floor and took in her space. "I get my very own bed, and I only have to share a bathroom with one other person now."

"And I can help you organize your bathroom when you're ready!" Margo said. Margo was very into labeling things, especially for other people. We'd spent two sessions discussing that.

"And I can help you organize your goals and dreams!" I added.

Shelley looked so much older. I couldn't describe how. She had on three necklaces. Her ponytail was cooler, or maybe her hair was shinier? When she smiled, there wasn't worry in her eyes.

She started unpacking. "I probably look tired. I cried so much last night."

"Because you were so happy you were coming

home?" I asked.

Shelley stared at me. "I had to say goodbye to Kukui. Do you know what it's like to look into a horse's eyes? It's like seeing into your own soul."

"Oh, I bet that was hard," Margo said.

Shelley nodded bravely. "Ezra and I went on a sunset ride with Aunty Inoa. Ezra didn't even talk to me. He's so good at knowing when not to talk."

"He sounds like a fantastic cousin," I said.

"The best," Shelley said. "I wish you guys could have a cousin like him. He made the summer awesome. And he taught me so much about horseback riding. I'm going to find a stable here now." She grabbed something from her bag. "Ooh, this is for you, Margo."

It was a snow globe, or maybe a sand globe, because it was Hawaii. Margo squealed. "Oh, I don't have any from Hawaii! Just New Zealand, Switzerland, Indonesia . . ."

"Proud to add to your collection. Oh, and here, Willis!"

She handed me two blocks of wood.

The blocks were gorgeous, with rich brown lines running down them. But I didn't know what they were for. Was I supposed to beat them together like old chalkboard erasers?

"They're bookends." Shelley laughed. "Made out of koa wood, which is only found in Hawaii. I thought you could use them on the bookshelf in your office."

I turned the blocks over. Engraved on one side was my name, "Willis Wilbur," and on the other it said "Life Coach."

What a treasure! This was the kind of present a VIP business person would get to celebrate a promotion. Someday a news show would follow me for a day to get a taste of all things Willis, and someone would pick these up and say, "This wood looks so woody!" and I'd brag all about my best friend, Shelley, who was gone for two and a half months but obviously never forgot me.

I hugged her. It was like Shelley never left, except it was better than her never leaving, because now I was friends with Margo, too, and the three of us were like a really yummy sandwich. (I don't know who is the bread and meat and cheese here. I'll figure that out another time.)

I was so happy, all sparkly and bright. It reminded me of the quote by Maya Angelou that said "Be a rainbow in somebody else's cloud."

I was just about to share that quote with my friends when there was a knock at the door. Mrs. Kalani poked her head in. "Hey, kids. The school just emailed your class assignments."

Ugh, I didn't have the cell phone today—Logan did. And it wouldn't even have mattered, because we had to share an old phone. My parents were trying to "responsibly monitor our technology," whatever that meant. Actually, it meant that Logan and I always fought over who got the phone on which day and anyway . . . Who cares! I needed to find out my teacher!

"Who do I have?" Shelley asked.

"Mr. Okoro," Mrs. Kalani said. "He's so great!"

Margo was already on her phone. "Me too! Me too!"

Then they all turned to me like email existed in my brain. "Who do I have?"

Mrs. Kalani looked down at her phone. "Hold on. I already texted your mom to check. Willis, you have . . . Miss Damour."

"Miss Damour?" The name meant nothing to me.

And worse yet, I wasn't with Shelley, who had been in my class every year since *kindergarten*.

"She's new." Mrs. Kalani smiled. "Moved here this summer, I think."

"Miss Damour." It didn't matter how many times I said her name. It never tasted right.

Shelley threw her arm around me and spoke low in my ear. "It's going to be okay. Okay? We knew we wouldn't have every class together for the rest of forever. We can still eat lunch together and hang out every day."

"Yeah. Totally. Yeah."

Margo and Shelley tried really hard to not be too excited.

But they *were* excited.

And I . . . I was dreading fourth grade.

CHAPTER 4

Logan's Destiny Switched!

Logan jumped on my bed to wake me up for the first day of school. "Willis! Willis! Come on, your destiny is starting!"

I rolled over in bed. It was 6:00 a.m. I didn't care about my destiny that early. Actually, I was ready to give up on my destiny altogether. I'd worked so hard to find it, but now that my destiny was clear—alone for a whole year without my best friend in my class—I did not want it.

That's right. I was refusing my destiny. And the best way to do that was to stay in bed.

"I still have thirty minutes of sleep," I said.

"This is the only time I can have a business meeting with you. Come on, I made you a power breakfast."

I put on my clothes that I'd laid out the night before—red pants, a blue button-down, a navy bow tie. Even though I was at school, I was still meeting potential clients every day. So I had to dress for success.

Logan had made me oatmeal and orange juice. She'd set the table and was in a cute romper with a new headband.

She also had on her lab coat, like she did every day for the last month. Look, I'm all about dressing the part, but what does a lab coat do besides protect your outfit from frog juice during a biology dissection?

Logan opened her back-to-school binder, which had index dividers. The orange divider said "life coaching," and the green one said "science experiments." I was both proud and jealous that she had so many things going on that she needed her life color coded. "So tomorrow you have an appointment with Adr—I mean, Client A."

"Thank you for correcting yourself."

"It's just the two of us. No one is going to find out about your *top secret* client."

"It's what he wants, and the customer is always—"

"Whatever. So Thursday you have a new client consult with Trista Mulligan—she's from my science camp. And we got two phone calls from that party, but one of them thought he was paying you to do his homework, so that was a no-go."

"Do you think Trista will want to work with me?" I took a bite of oatmeal.

"As long as you aren't mopey. Stop being mopey." Logan unclicked her pen. "Now, I'm looking at the books and . . . you need to start charging more if we're ever going to turn a profit."

I wasn't sure what *turning a profit* meant, but it

sounded important. "How much more?"

"You're only charging five dollars a session. And your spending is out of control. Did you really spend twenty-five dollars on gel pens?"

"It was a pack of fifty," I said. "And duh. I need pens to sign my name."

She kept pounding the calculator. "So you made fifty dollars."

Fifty dollars! That's a lot of money. "This week?"

"Like, total."

Oh.

Logan chewed on her pen. "You've got to find a way to charge more but still make it feel like they're getting a deal. Maybe we offer a discount if they're doing multiple sessions. Or have a punch card? Book nine sessions, get the tenth free."

"That's a great idea. Also, what do you think about doing a photo shoot? Then we can put a picture of me

32

on a park bench. For advertising. And I need more scented candles. Fall is coming, and vanilla pumpkin snickerdoodle *motivates* me."

Logan shut her binder. "Okay. We need to talk. I have good news and bad news."

"It doesn't *have* to be a pumpkin candle. I like autumn apple, too," I said.

"Willis, I can't work for you anymore." Logan brushed a hair out of her face. "That's the bad news. Well, bad for you. It's awesome for me. STEM destiny, here I come!"

"But . . . you're seven."

"So I have to be nine to get a destiny? Please." Logan patted my shoulder. "I'm giving my two weeks' notice. I'll start working on finding my replacement."

Don't ever tell her I said this, but Logan was a really important part of the Willis Wilbur brand. How was I going to get my own morning show without her? And what about when the whole family moves to LA for

Willis Wilbur Studios, my future movie company?

"And what's the good news?" I asked.

"You don't have to pay me fifty percent anymore."

"I was paying you fifty percent?"

She smiled. "How do you think I bought this nice lab coat?"

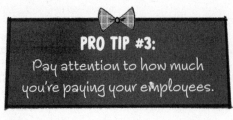

PRO TIP #3:
Pay attention to how much you're paying your employees.

CHAPTER 5

First Day of School!

I stood outside Miss Damour's classroom. I tried to remember a positive affirmation, but the only thing that popped into my head was

I don't want to go in there.

I don't want to go in there.

I don't want to go in there.

Which was getting me nowhere, literally. Finally, after another minute of deep breathing, I opened the door.

I knew becoming an upperclassman involved a

transition from little-kid education to big-kid learning. We were old enough to use scissors without assistance. We knew prefixes and suffixes. We'd started multiplication. But I was shocked how . . . empty everything felt. Gone were the vibrant bulletin boards I'd gazed at in third grade. Gone was the circle for morning announcements. The room didn't have much color at all.

And there was *zero* glitter.

Our desks were spaced in rows, which made me miss the tables we got to sit at when we were younger. I knew it was smart to distance students, but I hated walking in rows. There was never enough space, and sometimes I bumped into another desk, feeling clumsy and big. Worst of all, our name cards were already on the desks. When I became president of the World Wide Life Coaching Club someday (after I invented it), I would make sure that kids had choices in things that *matter*.

Like where they sat in a new classroom.

A short lady with a long braid came to the doorway. She wore a chunky necklace and swishy skirt. She smiled at me, but not a teeth smile. "Welcome to fourth grade! I'm Miss Damour. And who is this citizen?"

I didn't say anything because I didn't know she was talking to me. Her smile just waited. Finally, I said, "If you're asking what my name is, it's Willis Wilbur, upperclassman and life coach specializing in the kid journey." I surveyed the room. "Although I will occasionally work with animals or adults who really need help."

Miss Damour beamed. "I've heard about you, Willis. My cousin is on the BOO committee. She said you're a very hard worker." She thrust a bunch of papers in my hand. "Now, everyone is quietly filling out a detailed questionnaire. This information will help me as I plan our yearly course load, as well as the collective classroom personality. We'll share the statistics from this study soon."

I really wished Margo was there, because her spreadsheeting heart would love this lady. Or Shelley, who would agree that a little glitter never hurt anyone. I looked around the classroom. Not everyone was a stranger. There was Lyla, who always had the fanciest lunches with heart-shaped veggies or sticky rice. There was Ashton, who threw up during a jump roping assembly in first grade, but we all pretended like we forgot about it now. They were nice kids who would probably make great clients if I turned on the networking charm. But I didn't *know* know any of them, and they didn't know me, which made the whole statistics of fourth grade feel like lots and lots of work.

I got going on the four-page packet, which was very businesslike, but not in a fun way. Like I always left room for doodling on my client surveys—some people just express themselves better in doodles. But there was no room for anything but words, words, words. Still, I was pretty engrossed as the classroom filled up, until there were only two empty desks left, including the one next to me. I was about to lean over and see whose name was on the name tag when Miss Damour smiled and waved at someone in the doorway. "Hello, citizen! We're just about to get started. Find your seat, and I'll get you caught up."

"Sorry I'm late," said a voice that sounded sorta familiar. "I had to Zoom an emergency guitar lesson. That F chord is whoa."

And then the new kid, Colt what's-his-name, slid into the seat right next to me. He had on a gauzy cream V-neck shirt and a pink crystal necklace.

"How's it going, Beige?"

"It's Willis." I hissed the *S* sound in my name. "And I'm azure blue. Clearly."

Colt laughed. "True blue auras are deeply spiritual and calm. I'm not getting that vibe from you."

"You don't even *know* me."

"Sure." He shrugged. "But auras don't lie."

"Citizens?" Miss Damour stood between our seats. "I'm glad we're making friends here, but we need to get started."

"Fantastic!" I said loudly. I wanted to stop talking to this kid right away.

Which was new for me. I'm a big fan of people! And Colt wasn't mean, not exactly. So he called me a color. The wrong color, but so what? He was a person, right?

PRO TIP #4:
A person deserves the chance to show their true self.

"Do I need to separate you two?" Miss Damour asked.

"Willis was just asking me for advice," Colt said. "I get that a lot."

Me? Asking him? For advice?

Can you *believe* this kid?

"We'll all introduce ourselves in just a bit," Miss Damour said. "But first, we have a video announcement from the principal, who is very eager to meet you all."

I shifted my attention away from Colt like the professional that I am. Miss Damour flipped on the screen. Usually, the principal says something over the PA system like "Let's have a great year!" This was a very big production. Party music blasted through the speakers. The screen lit blue, then went into a whole animated intro with dancing horses and peace signs. Finally, there she was. Dr. Guinn. Our new principal.

Dr. Guinn stood in the auditorium with multicolor lights flashing around her and even a fog machine. "I am your new prince-ee-PAL, Dr. Guinn! Doctor, you say? What kind of doctor? A doctor of learning! A doctor of teamwork! And today, I'm here to share a huge announcement." Her hair was very, very curly and her lipstick was very, very pink. She smiled, revealing rainbow braces. Braces on an adult! Such a cool thing.

"She's too happy." The girl in the seat to my right wrinkled her nose. "And my dad's a dentist, and he says that only doctors are *real* doctors."

"When I die, I hope they put that on my tombstone," I said. "Too happy."

"Ew, why are you talking about *dying*?"

I know it's unprofessional, but I rolled my eyes. Some people will criticize anyone for doing anything.

The party music got quiet, and Dr. Guinn leaned in, her braces glinting in the light. "Today's a big day for all of us. The start of a new school year. And for me, it's even a new school. You know what I love about that? We are the makers of our own destiny. And that is what will be our theme for this year: Discovering Your Destiny!"

I accidentally gasped. Because what are the chances that I would have a world leader, well . . . a school leader

who recognizes the importance of destiny discovering? What are the chances that the school theme would also help me bring in many, many more clients? My legs kicked under my desk. And I did not look at Colt. I did not want to know if this made him excited or bored. I wanted to experience this all by myself.

"How are you going to do that?" Dr. Guinn grinned. "Students, we are starting off this year with a Passion Fair. Maybe that's a new word for you. Oprah Winfrey once said, 'Passion is energy. Feel the power that comes from focusing on what excites you.' That's what you're going to do! Participation is open to everyone. Working with a partner is encouraged. Maybe you love math and want to create a board of equations. Maybe interpretative dance is your thing? Whatever it is, this is your chance to pursue something you really love and share that joy with us in six weeks. Proposals are due in one week. And big news: The two passion project winners will go to the National Passion Fair in Washington, DC! So start dreaming, Green Slope Elementary!"

Dr. Guinn discussed more about the big event, but my head was spinning. I already had what is called "a leg up" on most of my classmates. I'd discovered my destiny months ago. Not to mention I had passion coming out of my ears!

Miss Damour shut off the screen. "You know, while we're all thinking about it, why don't you turn over your questionnaires and jot down a few ideas that you might have for your passion project. Just a quick brainstorm."

I didn't look at anyone else's paper. I didn't even look at anyone else's face. I was in the zone. My pencil flew as I brainstormed a million gazillion ways I could create a project around life coaching.

So my best friends weren't in my class. And Logan was looking at new career opportunities. And I had to sit by Beige Colt.

But honestly. This school year wasn't going to be as bad as I thought.

CHAPTER 6

The New Recess Schedule!

I had never been so excited for recess in my life. As soon as the bell rang, I ran outside so fast. I didn't say hi to my old teacher, Mrs. Harding, in the hallway. I didn't compliment the recess aide on her new hair color. There was no time. I had to find Shelley right away.

Of course, Shelley didn't rush outside as fast as I rushed outside, so I waited for her and Margo on the swings. We were still debating where our official recess spot would be for fourth grade. In third, we walked to the farthest tree on the sports field and either read books or played in the snow. In second grade, we were extra into four square (and by *we*, I mean Shelley), and first was lots of monkey bars. Ah, youth.

Shelley and Margo finally came outside with their class. They did not run like I did. Instead, I saw them stroll along, their heads bent low. They probably waited forty-eight whole seconds before they even looked up to find me. They waved and walked over.

"Ohmygoshwehavesomuchtotalkabout!" I said in one long breath. "Passion project! New kid. Rude colors. No glitter. Citizens! Logan quit."

"I've reserved the bench next to the softball field," Margo said. "Should we sit over there and chat?"

"Re . . . reserved?" I asked, still breathing deep.

"There's a system for upperclassmen," Margo said. "You can't just run over to an area and try to claim it as your own! You need to sign up. See how there are only ten students at tetherball? That's because there are only ten spots."

I surveyed the entire playground. Margo was right. There was an eerie order to everyone's play. No one was grouped into any one section. The swings had exactly enough kids. Same with four square. Even the kids who sat on the curb and read comics looked structured. "How did this happen?"

"I created an app," Margo said brightly. "It's called

48

Swingset. Everyone can rotate activities. Creates less injury and playground brawls."

"But . . . how?"

"I'll tell you all about it at our session." We arrived at the bench. Shelley looked around at everyone else. She probably was as shocked as I was that Margo had basically created an entirely new system of elementary school government and appointed herself as our ruler.

"So you said something about a new kid?" Margo asked.

"Yeah, look, I want to hear all about it." Shelley did not look like she wanted to hear about it. She didn't even seem like she was here with us. Maybe in body, but not mind. "Let's, uh, try and talk after school."

"Of course we'll talk after school." I slid onto the freshly painted wooden bench. I wondered, *Who would I need to talk to about posting an advertisement on here? Probably Margo.* "And we'll talk now. I have so many ideas."

Shelley's leg jiggled. "I bet you do but, um . . . I signed up to do some yoga with that group." She pointed at a cluster of very bendable kids on the far field. "Ezra and I totally got into yoga this summer. My body needs this."

Even Margo looked surprised. "But it's the first day of school. We haven't even talked about the lunch menu."

"I know, but I promised my new riding coach I would get my stretches in before practice today." Shelley was already walking away from us. "I can't wait to get back in the saddle. Ha, get it, Willis? Back in the saddle. Literally. Bye!"

She sprinted off, and Margo and I just sat there on that bench, staring as Shelley ran over to the group. Also, not a big deal, but Colt was over there, too. Yes, *that* Colt.

"Well, that was not how I thought things would go when I made this app," Margo said.

"Yoga!" I said. "Yoga? I could do yoga. I once taught a *guinea pig* yoga. I'm like the king of yoga. In fact, I could be a yoga life coach. I could host an international yoga retreat in Bora-Bora. I could out-yoga this whole school."

We watched Shelley as she moved into a cobra pose. You know what? The old Shelley I knew wasn't much of a joiner. Either her mom signed her up (softball) or someone else in her family did it first (clarinet). So this was actually pretty good for her, that she decided to do something alone. And wow, she'd *really* gotten into horses. Personally, they made me sneeze, but I was happy that she'd found something she loved. Just like I had with my business. No one could take that away from us.

Margo patted my hand. "It's okay. Let her find her own release. That's why I designed the app. By the way, can we just stop for a second and recognize how awesome it is that I designed a playground app?"

"It's very cool."

"I know. And it's an app for kids."

"Totally in the zone we worked through this

summer. You're a star, Margo."

"I am." She shined. "Now, you obviously have a million things to tell me. Pick one."

Here's the thing. As much as I liked Margo, she wasn't my *best* best friend. She was my really good friend. And when you have news or thoughts or possible changes, it's important to run those by your best friend first. So I had to hold on to my jumble of passion project ideas, especially since Shelley would obviously be my partner for whatever we picked. The more I thought about Logan quitting, the more I decided it might be a good thing. I went into life coaching partially because Shelley left over the summer. She was always so supportive and interested in everything I did. We emailed all the time, FaceTimed, the whole bit. So actually... offering her Logan's job would be an amazing way for us to spend more time together and build a fortune. Shelley could probably buy herself a horse in a few months if we put our minds together!

Which was why I couldn't talk about any of this with Margo right now. I didn't want her to feel left out. Fortunately, or maybe unfortunately, I had plenty to say about something else. "I have to talk to you about the new kid!" I moved to the end of the bench, like I was going to burst. "He moved here from this bay place, which I guess is in California. He sits right by me. He calls people colors. He thought I was beige, but I'm not. Oh, and get this. He offered to *help me*."

Margo's face scrunched up. "Wait, that guy over there with Shelley?"

I whirled around. Colt and Shelley were nodding their heads while they talked through a standing pose. Colt's hair was even floppier doing yoga. "Yes. How do they know each other?"

"Maybe they just met." Margo shrugged. "His name is Colt, right?"

"Ugh, you met him, too?"

Margo pulled something out of her pocket. "No. Someone in my class just gave me this."

It was a business card with very, very thick card stock. I knew it was expensive because I'd made my own business cards, and this paper was basically metal. Across the black paper, in gold letters, it read "Colt Whiting, Energy Coach and Healer."

Holy beige! Now this kid was my competition.

CHAPTER 7

My Top Secret Client!

I couldn't believe Colt had a business like my business. Obviously it was different because he was a healer, which sounded like an extra bold word to use. That part I wasn't worried about. It was that word: *COACH*.

There are lots of different kinds of life coaches—business, fitness, relationship, and according to Colt's card, energy coaches. I didn't know much about his niche, but I could guess it had something to do with all his aura talk. Other kids probably wouldn't know the difference between our coaching, either. Someone could even say,

"You should go to a life coach like my smart friend, Willis Wilbur," and the client could get mixed up and go to Colt instead. Colt would become a billionaire, and I would sit in my empty office wondering where I went wrong. This could happen. I mean, our last names both started with W!

I managed to get through the first day of school, but just barely. I kept my head down, didn't talk to anyone, kept my thoughts to myself—that kind of thing. By the time I got home, I thought I might explode from all the keeping-it-all-in, so I needed to practice self-care immediately. I lit a candle and watched my very favorite YouTube channel, which was created by local celebrity Michael Morales. His kid, Finch, was also one of my clients. That's confidential, of course, but still exciting to say.

Anyway, Mr. Morales's channel was on the Web of Business Success. (Some people think Success is a ladder, but Mr. Morales would point out some things happen at the same time or overlap each other. Also, you want to be a Sales Spider and bring the customer in. That was video three. You should really check it out.)

Okay, now that I've brought it up, so far he'd covered five parts of the Web of Business Success:

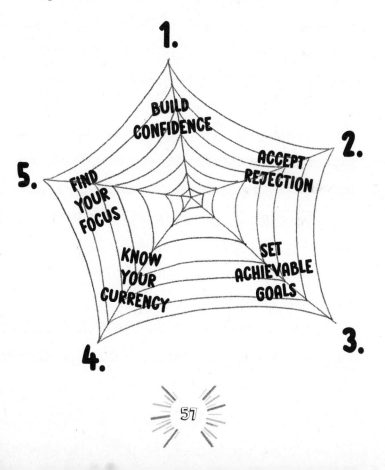

1. BUILD CONFIDENCE
2. ACCEPT REJECTION
3. SET ACHIEVABLE GOALS
4. KNOW YOUR CURRENCY
5. FIND YOUR FOCUS

The fifth video was especially helpful when it came to deciding my passion project. Other kids were probably starting at the very beginning. Like maybe they'd always wanted to build a birdhouse, so they needed to sketch out a design and buy wood and nails. But life coaching had so many different parts. There was the business side, the networking side, the clients side, the money side, the podcasting side, the scented candles side. If I counted it all up, there were maybe eighty-four sides. So I couldn't just fill out a form that said "Build a Life Coaching Empire." I had to find something new within my new career to really develop. The making-money part seemed appealing, since Logan said I wasn't doing that, but the *how* was haunting me.

Basically, I had passion coming out of my eyeballs. And I didn't know what to do with it.

My client today was VIP, big-deal, sorta famous. I sat in my office, which used to be the garage before my parents helped me make over the space and start living my dream. I had a little red clock that my mom got from Dollar Tree, and my leg was kicking in time with the seconds.

Someone knocked on the door. It was my VIP.

"Come in!" I called.

Okay, sure. I really hyped that up. And no—it was not Michael Morales or his kid or even the president of the United States. This was a local celebrity. More specifically—a Green Slope Elementary celebrity.

Client A, aka Adrian James. Remember how Adrian told his mountain biking friends about my life coaching business, but then at his first appointment, suddenly wanted our meetings to be secret (actually, you wouldn't remember, because I just told you)? Remember at the party how he didn't really talk to me? Remember how I handled this all like a true professional?

Adrian walked in and kind of sighed, like he was

releasing the burdens of the world in my safe space. You should also know that Adrian was super popular and extra good-looking and a year older than me so, like, an *upper* upperclassman.

"Hello, Adrian," I said. "I'm glad you could make it. Take a seat. Can I get you a water or anything?"

Adrian dropped into the large beanbag. "Nah."

"So what would you like us to be intentional about today?"

"I still don't know what you're talking about when you say that stuff. But I'm glad I had an appointment. I really needed to talk to someone."

I had to chew the inside of my cheek so I didn't smile too big. All my clients were important. Adrian was just, like, *very* important. "How was your first day of school?"

"Fine, I guess. No one whispered about me in class or put a sign on my desk that said 'Adrian is a bad reader.'"

"I'm not in fifth grade, but I'm guessing that never has happened ever?"

"Yeah, I know." He stretched out his legs. "How was school for you?"

"Stupendous," I lied. It's not my job to talk about me or talk about my friends or talk about my passion project or talk about the new kid or talk about Logan's lab coat. It was my job to listen, which . . . whoops.

"What do you think about that?" Adrian asked.

"What? Sorry, I missed that last part."

"I was just talking about all those tests over the summer. And I know having a learning difference doesn't make me dumb or anything, but . . . it's just new information. What if someone found out about it?"

We were jumping right in today! One strategy I learned from a life coaching book or maybe Oprah Winfrey was to repeat the same question back to the client. "What would happen if someone found out about it?"

Adrian shrugged. "Look, everyone at school has this idea of me. Like who I am or what I'm about. I don't want them to know I have a hard time with reading. Just like I don't want them to know I go to a life coach 'cuz I can't figure things out on my own."

I tried very hard not to correct him here. But . . . um, I failed. "Life coaching doesn't need to be a secret, Adrian. It shows that you are cool enough to better yourself. Also, you are an influencer. So it wouldn't hurt my business if you sent a few referrals."

"Yeah, nah." Adrian sat up in his beanbag. "I think the

way we are doing things now is good. Like secret agents, you know? Hey, can we do that UNO game where we talk about plans and dreams and stuff while we're playing?"

"Totally. But first . . . let's fill this chart out. It's about Facts and Stories. Sometimes we create these narratives in our head and decide they are a fact. Like you thinking everyone is going to find out about your learning difference or that they're talking about it. It might feel true, but it doesn't *make* it true. So let's separate some of these thoughts on two different sides. Facts or Stories."

I'd watched a video on this concept just yesterday, so I was excited to work on it with Adrian. We talked out where these thought patterns were coming from. We brainstormed ways to recognize them in the future so he didn't go down this whole path of thinking misbeliefs. It was pretty intense, to be honest, especially after all the energy used up on the first day of school.

After thirty minutes, I opened the desk drawer to

look for some cards. UNO Life Coaching was a game I'd invented to help get people talking and planning. I'd already written an article about my strategy. When I had more time, I would send it to the *New York Times*, who would publish it in their adult life section. Then I would get asked onto talk shows to demonstrate my technique. Then there would be the docuseries. Of course, my preference would be to include Adrian in all of this, but since he liked pretending I wasn't alive, that wasn't an option.

Not that I was taking it personally.

"Do you want to deal, or should I?" I asked. "And hey. I want you to know you're doing great work here, even if it's bit by bit. It's like Lucille Ball said, 'Remember to recognize the small successes.'"

Adrian laughed. "You know, Will, I wish I could keep you on my phone somehow. So I could just log on when I need a little shot of your weirdness. It helps."

In his phone.

Huh.

I once heard an author say they always get asked the question, "Where do you get your ideas?" It's hard to answer because ideas aren't candy bars you just buy at a gas station. Ideas come from everywhere, nowhere, or when different events smoosh together in the perfect way. If you added together this line from Adrian + conversation with Logan + conversation with Margo + video from our principal, it equaled something . . . something . . . wow.

I dealt the cards, but my head wasn't in the game. I was too busy thinking thinking thinking about my passion project. Finally I'd done it. *Find your focus.* And it was totally something I could share with my friends!

"UNO!" Adrian shouted.

Uno means "one." And this one was my best, brightest, biggest idea yet!

CHAPTER 8

A Back-to-School Tradition!

Every year we celebrate back-to-school by going to Don Pedro's Mexican Restaurant. We do not go on the actual first day of school, because that day is already busy enough. We order the largest bowl of guacamole, except for Logan, who orders a grilled cheese sandwich because sometimes she does enjoy acting her age.

We sing "Happy Birthday" to my dad, even though his birthday is still weeks away, because we like to double up our celebration. We buy fried ice cream. We're allowed to bring a friend. I have brought Shelley every year since first grade. Logan brings a new friend every time, and today she had a girl named Abby or Addy—I wasn't very sure, because she'd only said two words so far.

After they'd taken our order (and we'd eaten two bowls of chips), Dad asked, "So how was the first week of school for Shellis?"

Shellis was one of our couple names. We were also Willey. Also, we were not actually a "couple" and never would be.

"Incredible!" Shelley said. "I joined a yoga club. And I started riding at a new stable. Made some new friends there."

"Stable? I thought you played softball and clarinet," Dad said.

"I still do." Shelley bit into a chip. "I just found more passions this summer. My cousin got me into horseback riding."

"Awesome," Dad said. "What about you, Will?"

"I'm working on finding the positive elements of the academic experience," I said.

Mom sipped a frozen drink. "Did you pass out business cards, Bug? Or accomplish any of the other goals you charted out last week?"

I winced at the mention of business cards. Yes, I'd passed out more cards. So had Colt. The two of us still hadn't discussed our career overlap. We hadn't said much of anything to each other, except maybe "here" when we were passing out papers in class. Sometimes it looked like he was going to say something to me, but then I just ran to the bathroom or laughed to myself like

I'd remembered a funny joke.

PRO TIP #5:
Avoid your competition.

Mom bringing up business wasn't a bad thing. This was a nice way to start the important conversation I'd planned on having tonight. Except the food wasn't here yet. I wasn't sure if chips and guac were enough to fill them up before I dished out my huge news.

"Uh, yes!" I said. "I passed out lots of cards. And, uh, I actually wanted to talk to you all about something."

"I signed up for my passion project," Logan interrupted. "Abby is my partner."

"It's true," Abby said. "I'm her partner."

"We're not talking about you," I said.

"Our passion project is very time-consuming," Logan said.

"It's true," Abby said. "It's very time-consuming."

"I'm creating a home greenhouse with plant kits catered to environmental regions. I'll then market kits to kids so they can sustain a home garden in urban areas."

"It's true," Abby said. "She's creating a home greenhouse with—"

"Wow!" Mom cut in. "This sounds like an amazing commitment."

"Yes, I'll need lots of help," Logan said. "Lab techs, cleanup crew, stuff like that. I gave my two weeks' notice to my employer."

"Me. You're talking about me." I cleared my throat. At this rate, if I didn't shout out my news now, it was never going to happen. "Speaking of, I also have an amazing passion project proposal. Shelley, I'm so glad you're here, because this involves you."

Shelley lowered a chip she'd brought halfway to her mouth. "Me? What do you mean?"

I stood up. This was not sitting-down kind of news.

How often does someone come up with an idea that will . . .

1. make buckets of money,

2. give more resources and greater access to a large population of kids,

3. win the school spot for the National Passion Fair, and

4. globally change life coaching for everyone, anywhere, forever.

"I'm creating a Willis Wilbur Life Coaching App!" I announced. "It's sorta like a master class. I'll do mini video sessions so it's like I am life coaching kids in their own home. Shelley, you'll help with the filming and creative design, which is great because you're so creative and always so excited about my life coaching success. Margo made a playground app, so she can do all the coding stuff. Mom, you'll take everyone's money when they buy the app. Logan, I don't know if there's science involved, but I guess you can do that. Or I could really use some scheduling help if you have extra time. Dad, the team could really use some of your sugar cookies—"

Our waiter came with a big old tray of food. He set plates in front of us, annoyingly talking over me with phrases like "Careful, it's hot." My family didn't start eating their food. They just stared at me.

"That's . . . that's, um, ambitious," Dad said. "You mean, like, a phone app? Do you even know how to *download* an app?"

"You and Logan share an old phone," Mom said. "You couldn't even use your own app."

"Extra time?" Logan asked. "Willis, this is a full-time job. How are you going to coach your clients and go to school AND do this?"

"Wait, I'm confused," Shelley said. "You want *me* to help with this?"

Huh. I did not expect this mixed reaction, but that's fine. Sometimes it takes a while for people to recognize genius.

I sat down and turned to Shelley first. "Of course I want you to do this! I've been waiting all summer for you to get home so we can start building my empire. I used to think that would include you becoming a life coach, too, but now I see there are so many opportunities within

73

my business. Plus, I've got competition now with that pushy Colt kid moving here to energy coach. I really have to ramp things up, and I know you're the perfect person to help me do that!"

"Wow. Wow. That's . . . a lot to think about." Shelley bit into her enchilada.

"Willis. Honey." Mom reached across the table. "I love your gumption, but do you know anything about technology? Or about videos? Editing? Coding? Or even creating this much content? Maybe you could talk to a client I have who specializes in tech . . ."

Mom went on, but I didn't hear much. I was too busy thinking about all the fun in store for Shelley and me! Once I launched this app, we were both going to be millionaires. I could buy Don Pedro's, and we could eat lunch here every day, just us. Or she could buy her own horses! Here and in Hawaii. Margo would get part of the action, too, but I wanted to tell Shelley about this first, since she was my number one best friend.

Except Shelley wasn't saying anything. She just kept eating her enchilada like it was the most important enchilada in the world.

"Shells, I get the feeling that you are having different feelings than my feelings," I said. "Do you want to talk about that?"

Shelley put down her fork. "I'm just confused why you would do all this without talking to me."

"I wanted to surprise you."

"Obviously. But . . . what makes you think I want to do anything with life coaching?"

Now I put down my fork, totally in shock. Um, because life coaching is the coolest job in the world? And we could make tons of money? And actually spend time together? "Because . . . because *I'm* a life coach. And you're my best friend."

"But I have my *own* passions."

"I know, but we always share our passions."

"Look. I understand. We are best friends, and we do a lot together. I just . . . I wish you'd talked to me about this instead of pushing forward. I already have my *own* passion project. I turned in the paperwork to the principal."

I sat back in my seat, completely confused. I liked it better when she was eating enchiladas and not telling me weird news. "But . . . but how? This is the first I've heard about it all week."

"No, it's not. Margo and I talked about it at recess Thursday. I guess you weren't listening."

This was really offensive because I was basically a professional listener. Except, well, maybe I wasn't listening, because I had a lot going on. Also, I think I got ketchup on my scarf that day, which was really distracting.

The waiter came to remove our plates. Mom and Dad spoke in low tones to each other. Logan and her friend had drawn out a diagram of some sort on the back of a place mat. Partners already working together on their project. Sheesh, I was behind.

"Okay. Okay." I thought fast. There had to be a way to repair things with Shelley. "I guess . . . I guess I can do the app separately. I haven't turned in my sheet yet, so we can be partners for *your* passion project. What are we doing?"

"I'm working with an equine therapist. People connect with horses for emotional or physical healing."

"Whoa. Cool." This was already sorta my territory! My first client was an animal, which made me an animal life coach. So Shelley and I could work side by side, her with horse therapy and me, life coaching. Eventually, we'd develop a talk show, something like *Shellis in the Morning*. Could we bring a horse on set?

Shelley smiled. "It *is* cool. I'm taking a class at my stable with a few other riders. There's this one kid

I met at the stable this week. They're really into the healing nature of horses, so it felt like a natural fit to be partners."

I tried not to let the disappointment show on my face. All week, I'd just assumed Shelley would jump into my project. But it was really good that we'd both found passions. Some people live their whole life and never do! And I was happy she had someone to share this with. Really. Mostly. "Well, I bet there are still some neat chances for us to work together. Even if it's just to create posters or something. Does your partner go to our school?"

"Yeah. Totally."

"Do I know them?"

"Hmm?"

Just then, the mariachi band came over to sing to my dad. They gave him fried ice cream with lots of spoons. Mom smiled hopefully at me, like our tradition of embarrassing Dad would pick up my spirits. But I couldn't even pay attention to that, not with Shelley avoiding eye contact and guzzling her water. Like, all her water.

If I didn't know her better, I would think she was avoiding the question.

"Shelley? Your partner. Who is it?"

Shelley set down her drink. She let out a very long sigh.

"It's, ah, er . . . My partner is the new kid, Colt."

CHAPTER 9

Double Ditched
for Colt!

Shelley and I didn't talk much for the rest of the night. I tried, but anytime I started to form words, they came out as shouts in my brain. Stuff like . . .

HOW COULD YOU?

WHO ARE YOU?

REALLY? REALLY?????

So silence seemed like the best idea, at least until I'd processed the Icky News. Besides, I needed another person there to back me up when I told Shelley it was a bad idea to partner with my competitor. Margo would be firm, rational, and 100 percent on my side.

Luckily, the three of us already had a playdate set up for Saturday. I know, I know. Fourth graders having *playdates*, can you imagine? We all know that playing is our yesteryears and we are now in the zone of "hanging out." But our parents haven't gotten the memo, and I'm sure they are struggling a little with how quickly we are growing up. So if they want to call brunch in the park *playing*, go for it.

I brought hot chocolate and croissants from my dad's bakery. Margo had on a purple dress and Converse sneakers. Margo did not usually wear kid shoes like sneakers, and it felt like progress. She took the hot chocolate without saying anything and sat down on the fuzzy blanket I'd brought from home.

"Hello to you, too," I said.

"Sorry. I just need to check on the update I ran on my app." She whipped out her phone. Sometimes I was

81

jealous of her smartphone, but Margo obviously needed it, because she did smart things with it.

"It's fine." I stretched out on the blanket. "I haven't relaxed much all week."

"You and me both." Margo typed something else, then set down her phone. "Shelley said she told you about Colt."

I closed my eyes. Didn't I *just* say something about

relaxing? "I don't love that her partner is my competition. Or that she waited to tell me about it."

"Let's say you played sports." Margo lay down in the opposite direction so our heads were side by side. "And you played on one team. I don't know sports team names. The Fireflies? And Colt played on the, uh, Wasps. So you play in games against each other in your sport. Hockey. Baseball. Whatever. Would you be mad at Shelley if she played on Colt's team against you?"

"Of course not. You can't help what team you're on."

"Well, Colt and Shelley just happen to be on the same team when it comes to passion projects. It doesn't mean she is Team Colt for everything. And just because you and Colt are both coaches, it doesn't mean there isn't room for everyone in the field. You know?"

I did not know. She wasn't making sense. I wanted Margo to be really mad that Shelley would do this to me.

I checked my phone. There was a text from Shelley.

> Hey, not gonna make it today. Colt's mom got us into a stable in Colorado Springs. Driving now. Have fun with Margo!

I didn't say one word, just held up the phone.

"Okay. Never mind," Margo said. "I can't believe that team stuff I just said. Ugh, what's up with Shelley?"

I pulled myself up onto my elbow. "Right? Haven't you noticed that the Shelley who came home from Hawaii is different than the Shelley we knew last June?"

"She's never bailed on me like this before," Margo said. "I mean, she's already in the car with Colt. What are we supposed to do?"

"I don't know. She's our best friend," I said. "Best friends support their best friend when they start to like horses more than humans."

"That's true. But the support has to be mutual." Margo waited a beat, then unzipped her backpack. "I tried supporting the Colt thing. But I think we need to

84

go in another direction."

Margo held up a crisp piece of paper.

"Is that what I think it is?" I asked.

"Yep."

A Margo spreadsheet. The stuff of legend. The summary at the top was titled:

MARGO'S FOUR-STEP APPROACH TO RETAINING SHELLEY KALANI'S FRIENDSHIP

1. Do an activity she enjoys and pretend like you like it.
2. Remind her of all your shared memories.
3. Make something special for her.
4. Limit her contact with Colt.

"I thought we agreed you were going to cut back on these."

"Desperate times," she said. "Read."

Margo sipped her hot chocolate while I figured out the spreadsheet. There were multiple phases, colors, and dates involved.

"Can I make some changes?" I asked.

"No. You are either in or you're on your own. Please sign on the line at the bottom." She handed me a red pen. Once I'd signed the spreadsheet (who signs a spreadsheet?), Margo folded the sheet of paper and ripped the whole thing into little pieces. She promptly threw the spreadsheet in the trash can.

"Why'd you do that?"

"Evidence."

It was weird that I didn't like Margo a few months ago and now I was working with her to bring back our best friend. But life comes at you fast. This was an important partnership for both of us. Right now Colt was off telling Shelley she had a pretty yellow aura or something. Or they were talking about horse breathing making people

86

happier. Big bonding stuff.

"Are you sure this will work?" I asked.

"We might have to readjust it as we go along." Margo bit into her croissant. "But I get that this is a really big deal for you, Willis. Shelley has always been important to me, but we weren't tied together like you two were."

"We're still tied together."

"Sure." She checked her phone again. "Hey, if Shelley isn't coming, I should leave soon. Lots to do for my Swingset app."

PRO TIP #6:
Butter people up before
asking for favors.

"Oh yeah, speaking of apps. Um . . . I was hoping you'd want to work together on the passion project? I have a great idea."

"I already turned in my passion project proposal."

"Oh. Yeah. Okay."

I started packing up the food from the picnic. I had an extra croissant now because Shelley didn't show. Maybe I'd give it to Logan. Maybe I could work on her plant app thing with her. Maybe I would quit everything and find a whole new career, like farming, although overalls aren't my best look.

"Do you have any idea what goes into launching something like this?" Margo asked. "You are busy enough with life coaching."

"But I want to take life coaching to the next *level*," I said. "Can you help me set up the tech stuff? I can come up with all the ideas and videos that go on there."

"The tech stuff is most of the work, though."

"Pretty please?"

Margo grabbed the second croissant from me. "Fine. I'll create a template for you on top of my own app. I can be a private contractor for you. But I'm not going to get to it for a while. And this is a lot of work, Willis. You've got to figure out your affirmations and lessons and quotes and lists and all the stuff you do as a life coach."

"Who created his own business brand over the summer? Who created all my cool sessions that you totally benefited from? Who is the most famous life coach in Green Slope? Me. So have some faith here. Shelley will find her way back to us. Okay?"

Margo nodded her head. "Okay. I guess I can stay for a bit. Let's play on the swing set."

A tear almost fell down my cheek. My client who had to work on being a kid wanted to go "play." See? I was so good at this job.

That night, I rewrote the list Margo had created and ripped up, renaming it Get the Old Shelley Back.

I wrote an email to Shelley, just like we used to do in the old days (and by the old days, I mean two weeks ago when she was in Hawaii).

Hey Shelley,

I'm sorry for making life coaching plans that included you without talking to you about it first. I hope you had fun today with Colt. I want to understand your passions more! Can I come see the horses with you the next time you go to the stables?

Your best friend,
Willis

I didn't mean everything I said in the email (like I wasn't really sorry, and I didn't want her to have fun with Colt), but item number one was to do an activity Shelley liked and pretend like I did, too.

Shelley did not email me back. Instead she texted me, which was fine, but also, I sorta missed our emails.

I'm grooming horses tomorrow if you want to come with. But aren't you allergic to horses?

> I will take some allergy medication. And . . . is it just the two of us?

Are you asking if Colt is going?

> Colt? Colt. Hmmm I'm trying to remember. Do I know a Colt?

It'll just be the two of us.

Just the two of us.

Which was maybe my favorite thing my best friend had ever said.

CHAPTER 10

Shelley and Me
(and ~~Horses~~)!

"You can brush a new spot," Shelley said.

I lifted the brush from Spices's rear end. Spices was one of the horses at Shelley's stable. I'd been grooming Spices for fifteen minutes, and I'd already sneezed four times, even though Mom gave me allergy medication before coming.

"Where should I brush next?"

Shelley laughed. "Wherever you haven't. Her side. Spices loves being groomed. She's okay if you take all day."

All day? Who would want to be around sneezy, smelly horses all day?

I did not say that out loud because Shelley was really happy and chatty, and happy, chatty Shelley was fantastic!

"Kukui would get antsy whenever I groomed her. I think because she just wanted to be going, going, going all the time. Although she was also really obedient. Well, she's still in Hawaii, so I guess she still *is* obedient."

"Has Ezra sent you any more pictures?" I asked.

"I'll email you them later, ya?"

"Okay," I said.

Shelley frowned. "I love the horses here, but I still haven't made that special connection yet. Colt says some connections take longer to develop, but it doesn't mean they aren't meaningful."

Spices whinnied, so I moved my brush. She probably wanted to change the subject, too. "I'm sure you will make a best horse friend soon."

"That's funny. Colt said it the exact same way," Shelley said.

Here's the thing: I knew Colt was not Shelley's best friend. They'd only just met. So far, the only thing they had in common was horses. Shelley and I had a super-long history together. We'd even made it through the summer being away from each other. So I wasn't about to mess up my friendship with Shelley just because

94

I didn't like Colt hanging out with her.

But also—it kind of stung that Colt was saying things the same way I said things. Not just as a friend. I am also an original person, thank you. The only person who says things like I say things is ME.

I sneezed. Point one in the Shelley spreadsheet wasn't working. "Can I take a break?"

"Sure." Shelley led her horse into her stall. "Let's wash up and walk around a bit to give your allergies a rest."

"You remembered my allergies?" I asked.

"Duh. I remember everything about you."

This was the best best-friendy thing she'd said in a long time. I tried not to get too excited about it, but I couldn't wipe the huge smile off my face. "And you like frozen grapes, the color yellow, Taylor Swift, and that old-timey band your dad likes."

"Pink Floyd isn't old-timey! You're the one who loves the Beatles."

"You know me," I said.

It was a beautiful day. We walked up a hill that brought us to a grove of trees. Green Slope is really yellow in some parts and sometimes flat, but the stables were on the edge of a state forest that had riding trails. A few trees were already changing colors, and the air sorta whispered that fall was coming. Shelley and I used to go on more walks together—through town, through nature, through the neighborhood.

"Want me to show you the horse arena?" Shelley asked.

"Totally. I love the blue paint color they used."

"I love that you look at design everywhere, even a horse stable."

Which is totally true! And once Shelley pointed that out, I looked around for some improvements they could make. Although, I have to say, they had a riders' club room, which was a fancy sitting room with a fireplace and big rugs and pictures of old guys riding horses. And it looked fantastic.

We walked around the arena and talked about things. Just random things. We didn't finish all of our conversations, which was fine. We could finish or not finish them later. There was just too much to talk about. There were so many jokes to make and feelings to feel. I even stopped sneezing at some point. That's how perfect everything went.

Part of me wondered if I should bring up how I was sorta hurt by Shelley ditching us yesterday. She could have told us that she was missing the picnic way earlier than she did. Maybe even added a sorry.

But we were so happy right then together, and I didn't want to mess with the magic. I could just forget about it and move on to another phase in Margo's Shelley plan—the present phase. "Oh, I almost forgot. I ordered you this."

97

I held out a horse charm bracelet my mom bought at a local boutique. She paid for half, and I was supposed to pay Mom the rest later, but it would probably be *way* later because I still didn't have a lot of money. No worries—I was investing in friendship!

Shelley jumped up and down. Seriously, like a pony over a fence! That's how excited she was. "I love it! I love it. Oh, thank you, thank you."

Margo was a genius. The plan was going perfectly. I would keep doing the first three items over and over until I thought the time was right to get Shelley away from Colt. But right now, I didn't need to worry about anyone else. We were back in our best friend zone.

We were waiting outside for Mrs. Kalani to pick us up when Shelley squeezed my hand and said, "I'm glad you came today, Willis. I missed hanging out with you."

"Me too. I'm super glad you're home."

Someday in the future I would host a life coaching

event in that barn. Shelley would teach horse stuff to people at the same time. Someone would interview us, and the video would go viral because we are #friendsgoals. We'd each buy a limo but share one when driving to events together.

But that was later. In that moment, I was very happy that we were back to being Shellis. Or Willey.

In Session
at Recess!

I got to work on my app. Well, I sorta got to work on my app. Partly because I had no idea how to start . . . the *app* part of creating an app. But I had Margo! So the technology stuff would happen later. The content stuff I could do on my own.

I wrote so much every night that my wrist started to hurt. There were scripts and affirmations and advice lists (life coaches LOVE advice lists) and content, content, content. Content is basically all the stuff that people would be using and reading on the app.

And I was in charge of all of it!

I also calculated how much money I'd make, and let me tell you, it was A LOT. The app would be free at first, but then it would cost $1.99. Every time a kid downloaded it, I got money in my pocket! And eventually, I could add games and badges and stuff inside the app that kids would want to buy. Money inside the money! Not to mention more clients and exposure. The whole idea was one big win. I felt super hopeful when I turned in my passion project proposal a few days later.

Once that was done, I had to turn my attention back to business. I still had to give my clients the one-on-one attention that they deserved. Between schoolwork and app work and keeping-Shelley-as-my-best-friend, it was hard to squeeze in time with my clients. Which is why the recess app came in handy. Playtime became work time as I booked appointments on the bench, which was like my recess office. I even put up a little red sign that said

101

"Willis Wilbur, Playground Life Coach."

See what I did there? I'm the creativest.

Today I met with two of my semiregular clients, Spencer Limbaco and Ella Yorkstaff. These two had made incredible progress. They used to bully lots of kids (like me). But then they realized they were using bullying as a cover-up for their true feelings. For each other.

It's okay if you roll your eyes over that. Sometimes I had to wear sunglasses when I was with them.

Today they sat on the bench, holding hands like an old married couple. Ella smiled like she knew all the secrets in the world and the rest of us had baby brains. "So that's how our Habitat for Humanity date went. It was so meaningful to build a house together, wasn't it, Spence?"

"Yes, buttercup." Spencer beamed.

In case you're wondering, yes, I doubled their rate because there were two of them. And it still didn't feel like enough money.

"Wow, that's a great summary," I said. "What did you decide to do for your passion project?"

"We were thinking water filtration systems," Spencer said. "Do you know how many people live without clean water? My uncle James has a nonprofit that provides clean water for developing countries."

A ball bounced on the grass, nearly bouncing into my lap. I threw it back at the soccer players without taking my eyes off of my clients. "That sounds so meaningful. How will you work with the organization?"

"They need help doing social media. Posting pics and stuff. Also, Spencer's designing this app—"

"An . . . app you say?" Hmmmm, volunteering is a great passion project, but maybe they could take a break from being better people to work for me! I could really, really use the help. I would have to set a rule about not holding hands, though. "Let's talk more about that."

A whistle blew and we all looked over, but it was a warning for a kid trying to climb a fence.

"I don't know about this recess life coaching, Walr—sorry." Ella almost used a mean nickname but stopped herself. "There're too many distractions here."

"Totally," I said. "Now, what were you saying about an app?"

"I'm proud of you for correcting yourself," Spencer said.

"Thank you, schnookums," Ella said.

I squeezed the edge of the bench. I just couldn't with these two. Could not.

104

"Let's get back to what you know about building apps," I said. "Do you do consulting? Or would you take a contract? I'm hoping to launch by next week so—"

"Wait, what are you talking about?" Ella asked.

"Oh, I'm just...designing an app, too. For my passion project. And I thought I'd give you an opportunity to make some extra money."

"This *is* a passion project!" Spence said. "We're not in it for the money. And please stay focused. Ella was just saying that these recess sessions aren't working for us."

"Thank you." Ella cleared her throat. "Colt told me that innovation happens when you're comfortable in your environment."

I'd gotten used to this. Colt had somehow made best friends with everybody in the entire universe. I couldn't get mad about some silly comment he probably made while they were in line for the bathroom. "Oh yeah. That Colt guy. He sits by me in class. How do you know him?"

Spencer and Ella looked at each other like I'd just caught them in something. And suddenly, I felt very strange.

"Seriously. How do you know Colt?"

"He's just helping us mesh our energies," Ella said.

"You're . . . working with him?" My voice came out low. Angry.

I'd seen the business card. I knew this was a possibility. But . . . not really? Because I also am very good at my job. So good that there was no reason to go to a healer or whatever Colt was and have him *mesh energies*.

Ella and Spencer once egged my house, which was obviously Not Cool. But working with my competitor was even worse! Colt clearly had zero professional boundaries. This guy needed to stop stealing my clients, not to mention my best friend. Things had crossed a line. How was I the only one seeing that?

I looked over at the yoga corner. Colt was standing

106

on his head. I wanted to push him over.

"Sorry, I need . . . to pause our session." I stood up. I was going to march right over to Colt and invite him to a nice business brunch. I would bring my dad's quiche. We would set some professional boundaries and maybe even agree that he would *not* give advice to my best friends or clients or really anyone in Green Slope. This was my territory and *enough was enough!*

But brunch with Colt never happened. Instead, my whole plan was smacked in the face. Literally. There was this whistling sound, then my head sorta exploded and then everything was just . . .

Dark.

CHAPTER 12

My Principal Is a Penguin!

I licked my orange sherbet ice cream. Orange sherbet always tastes good, but it was especially good today. That's probably because:

1. Miss Stacey, the cafeteria lady, sent me the cone.

2. She sent me the cone so I could compose myself before going to math class.

3. I wasn't in math class because I was in the nurse's office.

4. I was in the nurse's office because someone kicked a soccer ball in my face.

5. Someone kicked a soccer ball in my face because I wasn't paying attention because, as you will remember, Ella and Spencer had just told me they'd betrayed me by going to my competitor for energy meshing, and I was about to walk over and give that scheming, tricky, business-thieving Colt a big old piece of my mind!

PRO TIP #7:
Avoid projectile objects in your workspace.

My face looked worse than it actually felt, so I was soaking up all the attention from the office staff. I HAD planned on taking some new professional headshots this weekend, but this swollen nose and a black eye meant they would have to wait.

Mrs. Kalani, Shelley's mom, was the school nurse, so if there was ever a good time to take a soccer ball in the face, this was it. Mrs. Kalani knew important tricks like using crushed ice instead of big cubes.

"How are you feeling?" she asked. "Never mind. I know the answer. Not great."

"Not great." I licked my ice cream, which hurt my face, but to be honest, it was pretty numb, anyway. Also, I was still coming off the drama of it all. I swear the entire playground was circled around me when I regained consciousness. I bet everyone was back in their class talking about it right now. Maybe they were even holding a candlelight vigil or a celebrity fundraiser to help me pull through this.

"Once you feel up to it, Principal Guinn wants to meet with you."

My ice cream froze in front of my face. "Okay. That would be great."

After I rested for fifteen more minutes, Mrs. Kalani brought me into Dr. Guinn's office. Dr. Guinn was in there, wearing a gray sweater and red leather sneakers. Her office was decorated better than any office had ever been decorated.

"Willis Wilbur! Here in the flesh!" she said.

I motioned to my face. "Oh, I stopped bleeding."

"That's great!" She walked around her desk. "Isn't it awesome that our bodies can heal themselves? But 'in the flesh' just means in person."

"Oh. Okay." I smiled. Which kind of hurt. "Then yes. Pleased to meet you."

111

"Willis is practically one of my own," Mrs. Kalani said. "I thought it best that he sits in here so the other kids don't see his face."

"Do I look that bad?" I asked.

Mrs. Kalani just patted my head and left the door open behind her.

Dr. Guinn motioned for me to sit in the scratchy tan chair with a fluffy purple pillow covering it. There was a lot of color in this room. A whole rainbow of color. And penguins! Not actual, alive penguins, but little statues and paintings and bobbleheads. There was even a penguin picture frame with Dr. Guinn and another lady standing on a mountain.

"My wife and I hiked Kilimanjaro," Dr. Guinn said.

"That's neat," I said. "But can you please explain the penguins?"

She sighed. "My first name is Penelope. Sometimes people call me Penny. So Penny Guinn. Penguin. It's very hard to lose a nickname like that."

"I understand. Some people call me Walrus instead of Willis. Except that's because of my size. You don't look much like a penguin."

Dr. Guinn stared at me, maybe because I mentioned my weight. I don't talk about it a lot, but other people do, so why can't I say anything about my own body? I'm not ashamed of it. It treats me well—except for the blood that started trickling down my nose again. I grabbed a tissue.

"You know, John Lennon from the Beatles wrote a song called—"

"'I Am the Walrus,'" I said. "I know. But I can't think of any famous people with a penguin song."

"We would both do well in the arctic. How many people can say that?" Dr. Guinn stuck her elbows on her desk. "I'm sorry about your face, Willis, but I am glad I have this opportunity to talk to you. I read your passion project proposal."

"Oh, really?" I perked right up. This was the moment when Dr. Guinn would tell me that I'd already won the Passion Fair based on my proposal alone. In fact, she wanted the two of us to fly out to New York City to share the app with investors. We would change the name to Penguin and Walrus Life Coaching, or maybe just Arctic Advisors. She would probably come up with those details—principals were great at administrative decisions.

Margo would need to fly out to meet with web

designers and computery people, but Dr. Guinn and I would be the face of the business. Once my face healed, of course! I hoped Dr. Guinn would give me enough time to heal. Otherwise, we'd have to get a really great makeup artist for our photo shoot for the cover of *Tech Universe* magazine (which might not be a magazine, but if it's not, we could create that, too).

"I think it's a very ambitious project," Dr. Guinn said.

"Thank you," I said

"Maybe . . . too ambitious?"

"I don't understand," I said.

Dr. Guinn stood up and started pacing behind her desk. I tried not to watch her, because the movement made me dizzy, especially with all the penguins around the room. "Life coaching is, well, there's a lot to it. Not only do you have to invest in the concept, there's so much to learn about business. Adults study years to become a coach. My own coach took a Buddhist vow of silence for a season. Then you add the technology component and . . ."

I held out a hand. "Excuse me, Dr. Guinn?"

She stopped pacing. "Yes?"

"I'm so excited that you have a life coach of your own. And whew! You are right. There's so much to learn."

"Exactly." She smiled. "I want this to be fun, not overwhelming."

"But Dr. Guinn. I already *am* a life coach. I have eleven to thirteen clients, based on schedules. I've been in business for months. I've met many important business people, like Michael Morales."

"Who is Michael Morales?" she asked. Which is fine, because she was new.

"He's a big deal. His face is on park benches. But anyway." I changed out my tissue for a new one. "I already have a base. And I would build this app even without the Passion Fair. It's a logical next step."

116

"And you're doing this alone?"

That word, *alone*, was not fun. If Shelley had just done this project with me, I wouldn't have had to deal with that word. Or be quite as mad about Colt. Or Margo could have done it with me, although her situation I understood because Margo was the only person I knew who was more motivated than me.

"And you know you have to do this in a month?" she asked.

It did seem like a lot right then, but that was probably just because of the whole swollen-face thing. My normal face would be really confident. "In one month, I'll probably be a podcast celebrity, too."

Dr. Guinn looked at me for a very long time. Other people might be uncomfortable with the amount of time she looked at me. Part of the reason I didn't mind was because I really believed in my passion project. Also, I'd lost a lot of blood and was feeling a little dizzy.

"Okay, okay! I see that your passion on paper exists in real life, too. You have my support." Dr. Guinn nodded at me. "I'm very excited to see what you come up with, Willis."

"And I'm very excited to go to Washington, DC, for the National Fair." I stood up, keeping my bloody tissue in place. It was a perfect parting line, but then I realized my mom still wasn't there and Mrs. Kalani didn't want me scaring other kids with my face.

Dr. Guinn must have seen this because she smiled and said, "Any chance you like the game UNO?"

CHAPTER 13

Everyone's at the Library!

Mom took me to the doctor, but the worst part was the black eye. My nose wasn't broken, just tender. The doctor kept saying how lucky I was, since he'd "seen some scary sports injuries." I didn't bother to point out that this was an innocent bystander injury.

I tried to get work done on my passion project, but I wasn't sure what to do next. Margo still hadn't said anything about the tech part of the actual app, and I needed to film some sessions for master classes. *But* I didn't have anything or anyone *to* film, and I was so busy that my regular clients were having to wait a little longer for appointments, and this was all after Dr. Guinn tried to talk me out of doing this but I didn't listen, and now—well, I was sure everything would turn out fine because it had to.

It *had* to.

I decided one section of the app could be examples from my actual clients. I would record our sessions and then change the names and details and stuff. Another kid with the same problem might listen and think—oh, that works for me too! So I asked Adrian to meet me in the library for our next session. I booked a study room, which is a private room where you can talk without whispering, but there are still windows so it's not super top secret.

Adrian had on his basketball clothes, which was one of ten sports he played. His style was messy and cool at the same time, which I wanted to ask him how to do, but maybe later.

"Whoa," he said. "Look at your face, man."

"I can't look at my own face without a mirror, but I know. It's bad." And I still was mad about it. Mad at the soccer ball, but also mad at Colt for stealing my clients. And my passion project partner. And for calling me beige. I knew another kid kicked that ball in my face, but it still felt like Colt was behind all of this.

"I had a disagreement with a soccer ball, and the soccer ball won," I said.

Adrian snorted. He might've seemed intimidating to other people because he was so cool, but sometimes he wasn't so cool, and those times were fun.

I pulled out an old tape recorder and placed it on the table in front of us. "Do you mind if I record this session? I usually take lots of notes, but it helps me to be able to go back and listen. Plus, it's part of my passion project."

Adrian sat up straighter. "But you're not going to

tell anyone I'm meeting with you, right? I'm serious—it's not good for my rep."

"Right." And I wouldn't. Even though an Adrian James endorsement would be huge for my brand. Like, he could act in commercials for me. Or we could do a life coaching reality show. Adrian had that kind of star power.

"So catch me up. How are your goals going?"

"That's what I wanted to talk to you about. I need to pick my passion project."

"But the deadline already passed," I said.

He shrugged. "Dr. Guinn gave me an extension. I'm really struggling."

I tried to not have too much anxiety about Adrian being so behind. I had enough anxiety about *me* being behind. Even Shelley and Colt had two sessions together already (no comment!). And Logan had ten plants growing in the greenhouse backyard.

But everyone had to start somewhere, and I was

122

honored that Adrian would include me in his process.

"Do you have any ideas?" I asked. "We can brainstorm."

The study room had a big whiteboard on the wall. There were even new dry-erase markers that I made sure I didn't sniff, which was hard because everyone knows new markers smell like promise. I drew a big circle in the middle and wrote "passion project," then started drawing lines out of it for brainstorming.

"So what do you think? Robotics? Curing cancer?"

"Uh, I like biking?"

I wrote "biking" as one of the ideas because when you are brainstorming, no ideas are bad. (Even *biking*, I guess.)

"You're popular, which makes you an influencer," I said, writing the word on the board. "You could influence people to do something big and good!"

"Sure." Adrian looked right at me, like he was looking into my brain to get more ideas, which is not the meaning of *brainstorm*, but I looked back in case he got inspired.

Then Adrian looked past me and sort of waved at someone.

"You know her?"

I whirled around, and there was Margo in the big window waving at us.

"That's Margo. She lives down the street from you."
I turned off my recording device. I'd recorded enough of
Margo in our own sessions.

Margo yanked open the door. "Willis! Wow, your
face is still horrible. No offense."

I wasn't too offended because Margo sent me flowers
after the soccer ball incident. Shelley, however, did
nothing. Like, didn't even write me a note, even though
her mom was the nurse and one of the first people to
know about my injury. I didn't say anything to Shelley
because it's important to take the high road, but also, my
strategy wasn't working because I just got madder with
each day that passed.

"Anyway," Margo said. "My recess app is really
blowing up, and I need to make some big choices. I talked
to this designer who my mom knew when she lived in
France, and they are super on board with the app. Like,
they might want to *partner* with me. I'm not sure how

much growth my current business model—"

"Margo, I'm in the middle of something."

She stopped for a second, utterly perplexed why I wasn't instantly coaching. "What?"

I looked back at Adrian. He gave his head a little shake. I couldn't tell Margo he was a client, so she wasn't technically interrupting a session. And we were practically sitting in a fishbowl here. No one could see the board from outside the room, but they could definitely see us.

"Adrian and I just, uh, ran into each other in the library and were talking about passion projects."

"So you just started brainstorming. I can totally help." Margo slid into the seat next to me and studied the board. "Influencing, I like that one. How would you quantify that?"

Adrian looked like a squirrel who really wanted to find a nut, except that nut was not here. "Uh, well . . ."

"We need to get back to it!" I practically shouted.

"Thanks for offering to help, but we've got it."

"It'll be hard to narrow it down since you're so talented." Margo beamed at Adrian. Margo really liked to dish out compliments. So many that it made people, including me, sorta uncomfortable. "You have great interpersonal skills. I mean, you hang out with so many different groups. The Rudes, well the old Rudes, the indoor sports kids, the outdoor sports kids, the music kids . . . there's ten passions in there alone."

"Really?" Adrian sounded genuinely flattered. He got insecure about his learning challenges, thinking everyone noticed it, but no one did, and even if they did, it wasn't something to be ashamed of. I'd tried to go over this with him all summer, yet here he was, lighting up with one compliment from Margo. Which I guess was good, but *I* was the professional here.

"The hard thing really is picking just one passion," Margo said.

"You live down the street from me, don't you?" Adrian asked.

Then there was this smacking noise against the glass. We all jumped.

Logan smooshed her face up against the window. She blew on the glass. Shelley stood behind her. What was this, bring-everyone-you-know-to-work day?

"Willis, I need this room," Logan said.

"We signed up for it," I said.

She marched in with a big old stack of books. "Shelley and I are doing scientific research. You guys don't mind, right?"

Shelley hung back, not really looking any of us in the eye. "Logan, we can do our reading anywhere. Willis is in the middle of something."

And then I don't know why I did this. Part of it might have been because I was trying to help Adrian be secretive about his life coaching stuff. But another part of it likely had something to do with Shelley and the fact that she *still* hadn't said anything about my face, even though she was looking right at it.

I mean, we were the very best of friends, right?

I threw my arm around Adrian. "Okay, girls. You all need to head out. Adrian and I are . . . well, we're extra tight. We're trying to get our chill on. Just us two. Right, Adrian?"

"Yeah. Will and I are . . . hanging." Adrian didn't give any indication that I'd just acted like a total dork.

There was no way I could charge him my full rate for the day.

The girls all looked surprised, maybe even a little shocked. Like me saying I was friends with Adrian was the biggest news ever (which is pretty silly of Logan, because she *knew* he was secret Client A).

"You know what?" Logan said. "I need to go find some more books, anyway."

"Adrian, I hope you can narrow down your talents into one passion!" Margo said. "Call me if you need help making a spreadsheet."

And then it was just Shelley, who sat there chewing on her lip. Maybe she wanted me to include her? She used to be so good at doing that for me. I wanted to tell her that Adrian was a client, and I was hurt about the not-saying-anything-about-the-soccer-ball thing, not to mention the Colt weirdness. But I didn't have words. There was just this heavy air.

"Sorry to get in your way," Shelley said. "Guess I'll go."

She ran off. I whispered after her, "My face is fine, by the way!"

The librarian shushed me, so I closed the door and collapsed into a chair.

"Thanks for covering for me," Adrian said.

"No biggie," I said, even though my heart felt like this was a total biggie, and I didn't really know why.

Adrian doodled on a piece of paper. He looked at his artwork and scrunched up his nose, like he wasn't satisfied. Then he balled up the paper and tossed it into the trash.

"I can't believe you made that!" I said. "I never could do a trash basket toss."

"Really?" Adrian wadded up another piece of scratch paper and tossed it in again, easy. "I've made twenty in a row before."

Dr. Guinn told me that it was smart to keep your passion project simple. And what was more simple than doing that thing you were already good at? "Adrian, if sports are your passion, then what's wrong with that?"

"I dunno." Adrian shrugged. "All these other kids are doing science stuff. Look at you—designing an app? I couldn't do that."

I wasn't doing a great job at designing an app, either, but no need to mention that right now. "What if . . . what if you work it all together somehow? Reading is difficult for you, right?"

Adrian glanced around the room, like Margo and Logan could still hear, even though they were long gone.

"Keep it down."

"I'm just saying, maybe you can use one passion to become passionate about something else?"

"What, like read a page of a book for every free throw I hit?"

"I don't know what a free throw is, but yeah."

Adrian rubbed his lips, thinking. That's what you

want for your clients—tons of thinking. "Maybe."

It was time to wrap up this session while we were still on a high note. "Keep thinking about it. I'll help however I can. Now! Let's end with some positive affirmations."

Once I launched the app, I could just tell him to look up the positive affirmations part, but for now I pulled out my trusty spiral notebook and started looking for the perfect one for Adrian. "Okay! Let's do, 'I am passionate and progressive.'"

"I am passionate and progressive. I am passionate and progressive."

I smiled to myself. Adrian was going to be great at this. And so was I.

Now I just needed to channel all my amazingness into my life coaching app.

CHAPTER 14

Filming for
My Own App!

5 TIPS FOR A SUCCESSFUL MOBILE APP! (From *Tech World* magazine)

1. Sketch Your App Idea

Done! I started small with four areas—example videos, affirmations, goal setting, and well-being. I wrote out most of the affirmations and goal quizzes and found some cool meditation ideas, but the example videos were black holes. So I sketched a black hole on the idea sheet to fill in later!

2. Do Market Research

I spent most of the summer doing market research by working with clients. Unless market research means figuring out who would actually buy my app? How do you do that, ask everyone if they'll buy it? Isn't that bad manners?

3. Create Interesting Graphic Designs

Done! I am a wee bit artistic so I drew my designs and a logo and everything. Now I just needed to figure out how to get those designs onto the computer. Must ask Margo.

4. Build Your App with a Platform

What . . . does this mean? Isn't an app a bunch of words and pictures? Like, how do you *build* it? Must ask Margo.

5. Test for Security Issues with Sample Users

Must ask Margo.

With only two more weeks to get my work done, I had to do this thing called "compartmentalize."

This means you take some things in your life, put them in a box, and shut the lid so you don't have to think about them until later. So I stuck my friendship with Shelley into one box. Or maybe three boxes, because there were a lot of things wrapped around it— Colt, my face, horses. I slid those boxes under my bed until I could think about them later. Then I focused on the passion project box, which meant lessening my client load and doubling my content writing. There was also the heal-my-face box. Bruises don't look good on camera.

There weren't any actual boxes, by the way. This is called a metaphor.

I had most of the content for the app. Now I just needed that template from Margo. So I texted her. A lot. Like almost every day. I knew she was busy with her own app, but she *did* say she'd help me with mine. Finally, I got a text from her that said,

136

> I have a film studio booked for Saturday. Bring your scripts, props, costume . . . whatever. I'll get you the template then.

I put on my best polka-dot bow tie and added a blue scarf. There was no such thing as too many accessories on days when you look your destiny square in the eye.

Margo's mom had rented out an artist's loft for us to film my app videos. If you are wondering what artists' lofts look like, this one had a brick wall and big pipes in the ceiling and a green screen set up in front of a large wall. The whole space was a little echoey, so they hung a blanket along the wall. There were very large circle lights that they obviously used on movie stars.

"So, Willis. First we're going to film your introduction." Margo was in her director's chair, which was cool but annoying because I didn't get an actor/star chair. Logan was next to her, not wearing her lab coat (for once). "I need some makeup on his forehead. Too much shine."

Logan attacked me with a powder brush and even put some blush on my cheeks. My skin looked fantastic when she was done. Maybe I should start adding a little makeup to my daily routine. Shine is a real problem for us celebrities.

"You need to look at the camera," Logan said. "Because usually when you talk, you look everywhere."

"No, I don't."

"You're looking at the ceiling right now," Logan said.

"I'm thinking!"

"You are *connecting* with the kids watching. They are in the camera, not the ceiling." She stepped back and appraised her work. "I'm good at this, too. It's very hard having so many talents and not enough time to use them all."

"Willis!" Margo called. She had on a beret and a long button-down shirt. I don't know where she got the idea that this look said "director," especially since the beret kept sliding over her left ear. "I need you on your mark."

I stepped onto the green X taped onto the ground, thinking how this small moment was really just the beginning of many much bigger moments. There would be so many times in my life where I would go into makeup, or wardrobe. I would eat catered food or wait in greenrooms, which aren't always green but include celebrities waiting to do celebrity stuff like be interviewed. I would need to stand on marks and look at cameras and be miked. It's very complicated stuff, but I would do all this as the voice of my generation.

"Okay, so I'm going to ask you questions. You look into

this camera." She pointed to the main camera. Another one was to my right. "This camera will also film you. When we edit, we will switch back and forth so it looks like an interview. We won't include my voice in the videos, but asking you stuff will help you know where to go."

"Absolutely," I said.

"Try to answer without using too many *ums* or *uhs*. We can cut some out, but we want you to talk smooth."

"Uh . . ." Oh no! I was already doing it. "Um, okay."

"Just relax." Margo gave me a reassuring smile. "Have fun with this. You're going to be great. All right! Let's get going. Ready, set . . ."

"Hold on!" Logan ran over and fixed my bow tie. She squinted at me. "There's really nothing I can do about the hair, Margo. We just have to work with it."

"What's wrong with my hair?" I asked.

"And . . . action!"

The red light blinked on.

"All right, Willis. Let's start with a bit about you. Tell me who you are and how you got into life coaching."

Have you ever actually seen one of those TV interviewer cameras? They are not small. In fact, it looked like it could eat my whole face. And the light was very red. Is there a word for the color redder than red?

"Willis?"

I blinked. "Um . . . oh, sorry. Uh . . . Willis. Wilbur."

"Right." Margo made a motion to go on.

"Willis Wilbur. My name is Willis Wilbur."

"We got that," Margo said. "Tell us how you got into life coaching."

Not only was that one camera bigger than my whole body, but the other camera was also huge and documenting every move I made. Also, everyone in the room was *staring* at me. I gulped.

"I'm a life coach. I, uh, because I was at the doctor, like, uh, I broke my arm. Wait, let me back up. See, before that, there was a table and I was redecorating? Like, for my, uh, mom. And anyway, there was another table . . . not my mom's table, the doctor's table, and . . . um, yeah, there was a magazine. And then . . . wait, what was the question again?"

Logan jumped out of her director's chair and thrust a sheet of paper in my lap. I read it out loud. "My name is Willis Wilbur. I discovered my destiny of being a life coach, and now I'm here to discover yours." I looked up at Logan. "This is better."

"You could read the ingredients on a bag of potato chips, and it would be better than what you just did." Logan walked back to Margo. Their heads bent low as they whispered back and forth, occasionally gesturing to me.

Margo finally looked up and smiled. "We're going to try a different approach. Logan is making cue cards. So take a quick break, and we'll be right back with you."

The camera flipped off, and the cameraman, Margo's uncle Rick, stepped outside to take a phone call. I took some time to do some breathing after that rough beginning.

Breathe. Breathe. Breathe.

It was all fine. I would do better.

This was still my destiny.

I was confident and clear. *Confident and clear.*

Besides, we could edit all of the video later! The most important thing was to get all of this content into the app. Which I . . . I still needed that template from Margo.

I wandered over to the doughnut stand to very nicely ask for it. "This is all great. Thanks for helping."

"No problem," Margo said.

"It's just . . . um . . . remember how I needed the template for the actual, like, app?"

"Yeah, give me your phone, and I'll download it there."

"My old phone?" I asked.

Margo frowned. "Ugh, I forgot. Okay, your iPad."

"I don't . . . have one."

"Your laptop?"

"We have a home computer," I offered.

"I'll have to see if it's compatible."

"Great! You can come over right after this."

"Willis, I've been busy." Margo checked her watch. "Taking *today* off was hard. I'm doing a full overhaul on the Swingset app for these investors. I've been working on this for months. It's a big deal."

"That's so cool!" I nibbled on a doughnut, waiting a few moments. "So . . . tomorrow?"

"Fine. Sheesh, you are tenacious."

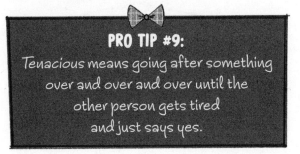

PRO TIP #9:
Tenacious means going after something over and over and over until the other person gets tired and just says yes.

CHAPTER 15

My First Interview!

Spencer and Ella held hands as they walked into the loft. I blushed for them, even though they didn't notice. Holding hands is weird because your hands sweat, and maybe one person has sweatier hands than the other. And also you have to walk at the same pace and maybe pretend you aren't even holding hands, even if you are. And *also*, also, you should use hand sanitizer before and after holding hands, which seems like a lot of work to just mix your hand sweat with someone.

"Hey, thank you for coming!" I waved them over to

the set. Yes, now we had an official "set" with a couch that Margo called a "love seat," a lamp, some flowers, and my nice distinguished chair. There was even a rug.

The throw pillows sorta clashed, but I didn't say anything.

"Glad to help," Spencer said.

"If we can help just one person, then we've done our job," Ella said.

"Sure," I said. Even though I was also paying them twenty dollars to be my example clients. Not to mention they'd gone to coaching with Colt, which I would not bring up today. Super mature of me, considering how much they'd betrayed me.

Logan and Margo decided to switch jobs for the second half of the day. They both looked tired, which was strange because I was the one who had to be on camera and looking good. Margo fussed over Ella's and Spencer's clothes. Their style was very "hoodie and Converse," which maybe wasn't actually a style, but they were clients so I didn't say that.

"Okay. Okay." I turned to Ella and Spencer. "So don't look at the camera when I ask you questions. Look at me or each other. This is supposed to be a sample life coaching session. In fact, really try to act like you would in one of our sessions. This will show other kids what it is like."

Ella waved her hand. "I was the teacup in *Beauty and the Beast*. I can do this."

"You were?" Spencer asked her.

Ella laughed. "Yeah, before I moved to Green Slope."

"You never told me you did theater," Spencer said.

"Is that a problem?" Ella asked.

"No, I just don't know why you'd keep that from me."

"I wasn't keeping it from you." Ella shrugged. "It never came up."

"Should, uh, we . . . start filming?" I made a note to not ask Ella anything about theater. Which was fine.

148

I had such a good plan to get back on track.

"Ready when you are," Margo said.

The camera light flicked on, and now that I wasn't alone, it wasn't so scary. "This is such a treat to meet with my fantastic clients today! Ella and Spencer have worked together to overcome some obstacles and become a dynamic pair."

My voice sounded so much more confident. I'd met with Spencer and Ella for at least eight sessions already. I knew how they worked and how they learned. Also, this was a much better camera angle for me. My face looked wiser on the left side.

"Ella, let's start with you. Why don't you give us a review of your highs and lows since our last session?"

Ella looked right at me and glowed. Seriously, she just turned on this light inside of her so fast it almost knocked me over. "Well, Willis. This week I really focused on listening to my inner child while still giving my outer self the chance to learn."

"How did that go for you?" I asked.

"Fantastic. My affirmations helped! It's important to remember where you came from. It's important to know where you want to go."

"So true." This wasn't scripted, but I patted the seat cushion next to me and said, "Would you join me in a quick meditation?"

Ella tossed her hair, which, now that I was looking at it, was pretty today. She usually had a hoodie on, so I didn't see it. In fact, she was dressed different overall. And I think there was glitter on her face.

We closed our eyes, and the room just hummed, and the camera was getting everything. It was perfect!

Afterward, I opened my eyes and turned to Spencer. "So, Spencer. Tell me what challenges you're facing."

"Me?" Spencer looked exactly the same as ever. Except maybe more confused than ever. "I don't know.

The same. Whatever," he said sullenly.

Ella patted his leg. "Sweetie, tell him about the passion project."

"I don't want to." Spencer's mouth was kind of . . . flat? Like, he wasn't smiling or frowning, but there was this creepy straight line.

"Why don't you tell us, Ella?" I asked.

"I feel like *Spencer* should say something, because he just shuts down when we talk together."

"At least I'm not hiding things," Spencer mumbled.

"We're meeting with Willis. On camera. Don't start, sugarplum."

"Start what? Having an actual conversation? And cut out the cutesy names."

"Now you don't think I'm cute?" Ella asked.

Margo peeked her head from behind the camera and started motioning to me, like she was making something blow up with her hands?

Oh. She meant this interview.

"Well, it seems that there are a few things we can, uh, unpack here?" It wasn't really a statement. Or a question. More like a cry for help.

Sometimes you don't think about how much is at stake until you face losing it. All my eggs were in this basket. All the time I would normally spend on my clients or growing my business had gone into creating this app. I barely knew what I was doing. But I really wanted to beat Colt. Wait, erase that. I wanted to be the best life coach in all of Colorado. I wanted to help.

I wanted these two to stop yelling.

"I was not hiding theater from you!" Ella stood up and threw a throw pillow at Spencer. "My mom has a picture of me on the wall from *Beauty and the Beast*. It's your fault that you never noticed."

"All I do is notice!" Spencer shouted. "And you're not leaving, I'm leaving."

They both stormed off the set. Margo flopped down on the couch next to me. "I could create a DON'T link for the site."

"At least they had passion," I said.

And then something extra surprising happened. We both burst into a fit of giggles, not because any of it was funny, but because it was so ridiculous. Also, we'd worked super hard and were so, so tired. Who'd have thought my "dream" clients would be such a nightmare?

"At least they didn't throw eggs!" Logan called.

Then we laughed even harder. I made sure not to cry, though, because again, my makeup really did look great.

153

CHAPTER 16

The Decorating Committee!

Margo added the app template to my home computer. It was designed so I didn't have to do any coding—just add my content into the program. I kind of wanted Margo to add all the content for me, but she said she hadn't really slept in days and needed to go home. Which was fine—she'd delivered on her promise, and as soon as I got a second, I would input it all and . . . voilà! App Superstar!

But first I had to button up a few things. Like the next day, when Miss Damour called me up to her desk.

"Willis, Dr. Guinn has asked each teacher to send three volunteer citizens to set up the Passion Fair on the cafeteria stage. Would you be interested in helping?"

I almost hugged Miss Damour. First, I was flattered that she recognized my leadership abilities. Second, there was a very good chance that Margo would also be selected, and I had more app questions. Third, I wanted to get out of our geology unit because Colt knew *soooooo* much about minerals and crystals. "It would be an honor!"

"Great. You can catch up on any work you miss later. Head on down to the cafeteria with Colt."

"I'm sorry, what?"

Miss Damour pointed to Colt, who was already standing at the classroom door. "I also selected Colt and Fiona. You can walk down right now."

Fiona had already left, which I hadn't noticed

because sometimes I only notice things that matter to me. So it was just Colt and me walking down the hallway. Together.

"So how's your passion project going?" Colt asked.

"Divine!" I may have had too much enthusiasm in my voice. It was better than all the other feelings I had for Colt. I wondered if he had any clue that he was ruining my life.

"Yeah, Shelley told me about your app," he said. "Sounds like a cool resource. I'd love to use it with my clients."

I know it sounded like Colt was giving me a compliment. But also the fact that he had clients was not really a compliment? Because some of those clients were *my* clients?

But I was a classy kid. I straightened my shoulders. "How is . . . your project going?"

"I'm sure Shelley told you all about the disaster with

the American quarter horse."

"Oh . . . yeah. That was something." She had not told me anything. We hadn't really talked in a few days. Maybe a week. Which hurt. A lot of this hurt.

Colt stopped walking and put a heavy hand on my shoulder. "Hey, do you want to talk about your energy?"

We were so close to the door of the cafeteria. *So* close. "Not . . . really."

"It's just . . . I'm an empath, you know? Which means I have a higher sense of perception. I can feel that you're really going through something, Willis Wilbur. Would you like me to work with you to heal?"

"*You* want to work with *me*?" I asked. "As my coach?"

"Totally. We've got some synchronicity here. Even life coaches need coaches."

I didn't say a word. There were no good words to say. I just turned and walked straight into the gym.

157

Setup had already started. Large sheets of colorful butcher paper were twisted around the entrance of the stage, giving a curtain-like effect. There were large red flowers and swirling twists of yellow and purple. Volunteers worked together to add tape to the paper to attach to the walls.

Margo was nowhere to be seen, which was bizarre because when it came to school things, Margo was everywhere, always. Shelley was there, though. She gave me a little wave when I walked in. I pulled my scarf tighter around my neck and did some deep breathing. I know I said I didn't have time to open the Shelley box, but it was a big box that was right there in front me. Plus, I still remembered the last item on Margo's get-Shelley-back list. *Limit Shelley's contact with Colt.*

Time was ticking! I ran up to Shelley and grabbed her hand.

"Come get a snack with me!" I said.

"What?" she asked. "Willis, what's happening?"

"We need carbs. And bonding. Come on."

I dragged her into the hallway before Colt could even see us.

Our school vending machine was in the courtyard. A few years ago, there was a fifth grader, Alma Suiz, who ran for student body president. Her campaign promise was that she would get a healthy vending machine. And she actually did it. I think about her sometimes when work is hard. If Alma could talk the PTA into a vending machine, I could do anything, too.

So anyway, Shelley and I stood there contemplating our healthy options. I knew she usually got a fig and honey granola bar, just like I usually got chickpea chips. But so many things had changed, and I wasn't sure if her treat was still her treat, you know?

Shelley punched in the numbers for her old favorite granola bar. I actually breathed a sigh of relief.

159

"So what's up?" Shelley asked.

I didn't have a plan of what to say to her. I'd never needed a plan when it came to Shelley. We just were. But we'd let a distance grow between us. If I wanted to reconnect, I needed to swallow my pride.

So she hadn't said anything about my bruise. She was really busy. It didn't mean she was mad or didn't like me, right? It didn't mean we couldn't get back to how things were?

"Nothing. Wow, we've both just been so busy that we haven't talked in forever. I'm so glad we both get to work on decorating."

"I think my mom told Dr. Guinn I'm good at paper flower making." Shelley laughed. "I didn't really have a choice."

"Oh. Ha. Yeah."

"So how is your passion project going?" Shelley asked. Which was great, because my mind had forgotten how to have conversations. "Logan said your video with Spencer and Ella looked really professional."

"Yeah, thanks." I hoped my smile wasn't as stressed as I felt. "The app is still . . . a work in progress."

"Do you need help?" Shelley asked.

I stared at her. "Really? You'd . . . help me?"

Shelley put her hand on my shoulder. "Look, things have been weird, right?"

"Right."

"But, like, why?" She stared at me expectantly, like I had the answer.

Here's the thing about life coaching. I did not have

all of the answers. Lately, it just felt like everything was a question. So I certainly couldn't figure out where we'd gone off course.

PRO TIP #10:
Even when you're not sure about your feelings, try to be honest about them.

"I don't know what happened with us," I said truthfully. "But I don't like it."

"There you are!" Colt called across the courtyard to Shelley. "I've been looking all over! Shells, they need help twisting the flowers."

"I'll be there in a bit," Shelley called.

Shells? Did he just yell my nickname for Shelley across the courtyard?

The problem was obvious. I was *this* close to blurting out that Colt was the thing that had changed us. He had inside stories about horses with her. They hung out all the time. He probably energy coached her or used his empath skill, whatever that was.

But I wanted to keep things cool between us. So I just asked, "How's your passion project going?"

"Colt is positive we're going to win the whole thing."

"Uh-huh." I punched my treat numbers into the machine. Horses and therapy are neat and all, but did Colt really truly think he was going to beat *everyone*? "Colt seems . . . really confident."

"Yeah. It gets annoying sometimes," Shelley said.

I'm pretty sure my ears literally stood at attention. This was new. It felt like my first opportunity for Margo's plan, part four. "Oh yeah? How?"

"He's just so into the passion project that his focus is more on that than the horses." Shelley started walking back to the cafeteria. I followed her. "And I think equine therapy is important, but also I want to ride as much as I can. You know?"

"That's really hard." I'd slowed my pace so I could maximize this moment. "Like, you care about the passion project, but you don't want to lose your riding time."

"Exactly!" Shelley grinned. "Plus, he doesn't always get my jokes. And if I have, like, a crick in my neck he wants to help heal me right away. I don't know. He's a nice kid. I think he's really just lonely."

"Colt? Colt . . . Whiting? Floppy hair kid, always reading auras?"

"He's new. He's trying." Shelley sighed. "He doesn't have long friendships like me and you."

My heart warmed up a bit at the mention of our super-long friendship. "I hadn't thought about that."

"I just think he's trying hard to be so busy that he doesn't have be alone. Even though he meditates all the time. He just doesn't know how to be by himself."

Honestly, in that moment, she could have been talking about me instead of Colt. Who has time to just sit around and BE? How boring. There's too much to achieve! Although Shelley's always been more that way, and I've been more this way. Which doesn't matter because the true moral of the story is: She's not best friends with Colt!

"Are you coming to Colt's party on Saturday?" Shelley asked.

Oof. The party. I knew about it, but I hadn't read the invitation because I threw it across the room. It was a bad day, okay?

"I haven't decided."

"You won't want to miss it. Everyone is coming." We made it to the cafeteria. Colt was talking to Margo. See? I knew she'd show up to help. Even from across the room, she looked . . . unkempt. She had a blazer on, but the buttons didn't match up. Her glasses were a little crooked. And she was gesturing a whole bunch with her hands. Maybe she'd started something super adult, like drinking coffee?

"Is she okay?" Shelley asked.

"Margo? She's always okay. She was at my house just yesterday setting up my app template."

"You . . . haven't done that yet?" Shelley asked.

"It's pretty much done." Or not done at all but, like, ready to be done.

"I would drop everything and just focus on that. Something could still go wrong."

"Thanks for the advice!" I said. It was sweet that Shelley was worried—it showed that she cared. But I had a renewed optimism that everything was going to turn out great! Miss Damour had just recognized what a star student I was. Shelley knew Colt was the worst and would stop talking to him as soon as the project was done. I was an hour on the computer away from launching an app.

I just had to get through another week of hard work and then everything would be back on track for Willis Wilbur!

CHAPTER 17

Colt's Energy Party!

Colt's party invitation advertised an "Energy Experience." I had oodles of energy, so I didn't really need it, but I also knew everyone else was going and didn't want to miss out. Even Logan was going. With me. Which was a little annoying.

Dad dropped us off at Colt's house, which was up in Green Slope Hills. Green Slope is in a little valley in the Rocky Mountains, so there are a lot of hills. But Green Slope Hills is a super-nice neighborhood, where all the celebrities would live if celebrities lived here.

Michael Morales lived there.

The house had lots of big windows and sharp lines. It was built into the mountain and had this spectacular view of the reservoir and city and everything. Totally the kind of place I would live someday. Totally not something I would tell Colt.

Logan rang the doorbell. "This place is so cool. Can you believe how cool Colt is?"

"I mean, his parents have nice architecture taste. I don't think that makes their son cool."

Logan played with the hem of her shirt. She didn't have her lab coat on, and she'd done her hair differently. It was like . . . It was like she really cared about this party.

An adult answered the door and kind of bowed at us. "Well, hello! I'm Colt's mom, Mindy."

Logan did a curtsy. Like an honest-to-goodness curtsy. "I'm Logan Wilbur. This is my brother, Willis. Thank you for inviting us into your home."

Colt's mom grinned. "What fabulous manners. And your aura is just glowing! Come on back. I made some hummus. Oh, and please take off your shoes."

The house was oddly quiet considering there was a party going on. You could hear our feet against the cement floor.

"Did you know Colt went to a camp in California that taught him everything about energy work?" Logan asked. "You never went to a camp for life coaching."

169

"I'm certified!" I said.

"Not *camp* certified." Logan sniffed.

"Doesn't mean I'm not good. You'd make a great life coach, too. In fact, I bet you could life coach your plants. Talk to them, sing to them. That kind of stuff."

Logan scratched her chin. "It's not the worst idea you've had."

We came to the large living room that had one whole side of glass windows. Expensive art hung on the walls. The couch alone was the size of our TV room. Our classmates were twisted in various yoga positions. Flute music played in the background.

Shelley finally saw me when she moved into downward dog. "Willis!" She patted the mat next to her. "I saved you a spot."

I was not in yoga wear. My blue pants were not bendy, plus there was the bow tie. I sat down cross-legged next to Shelley. "I didn't know this was a retreat."

170

"I just think this is Colt's style, you know?" Shelley moved into another position. I have to say, it's a little weird that she hadn't told me more details about this party. In the past, we would have talked a whole bunch before it started. We would have coordinated our outfits. We would have come here together.

But we were still together. I had to remind myself of that. We were talking and laughing again. I was here so I could see Shelley. I was here to reunite Shellis.

Colt's mom clapped her hands, and everyone stopped twisting. There were a lot of people here—like thirty or forty. It was a REALLY big living room. Margo was over by Adrian, and Ella and Spencer were here, but not by each other. And there were other kids I'd tried to get as clients who'd never seemed interested. I'd thrown some mean parties in my day, but this was a bash.

"Thanks for coming!" Colt's mom said. "We've set up

some stations for everyone inside and outside."

Colt stood next to her. He had on a really deep V-neck and some funky yoga pants. He also had a crystal necklace that was . . . Okay, it was really cool. "Thanks, Mom. Yeah, you'll see there's a nutrition station. Enjoy some cucumber water and Mom's organic hummus. There's also a crystal display—read the different descriptions and pick one crystal that really speaks to you. I'll be reading auras outside. Or you can find a quiet spot and meditate. I want everyone to feel at home here, K?"

"Colt's mom is so cool," Shelley said in my ear. "Did you know she's traveled the world teaching yoga? Colt said she can help me improve my breathing. Like, I am always holding my breath."

Remember when we were at the vending machine and Shelley mentioned that Colt could be annoying? Where was that feeling now? Here it was just Colt, Colt,

Colt everywhere I looked. "Which station do you want to do?"

"Oh! Crystals."

We went to the table outside. It was a pretty day, but nothing *felt* pretty. Maybe I was bothered that Shelley had switched on her enthusiasm for yoga, Colt's mom, all of this. Maybe I was sad that he had such a great turnout when I only had a dozen clients myself. Maybe I was starting to worry he would actually win the Passion Fair and take over the whole school. Take over every dream I'd ever dreamed. I don't know.

"You need to come back to the stables soon," Shelley said. "At least to meet the kids we're working with— I think they could be clients for you, too."

"Uh-huh." I picked up a yellow stone. Colt's mom had handwritten little cards identifying each pile of rocks. She'd also written a list of properties for each stone. Yes! It was very cool. No! I was not admitting that.

I rubbed a sleek gray rock that had a sort of silvery shine to it. Hematite. Super slippery, in a good way.

May help to restore peace and harmony in the body the card said.

I put it in my pocket.

"Did you ever thank Margo for doing so much work on your passion project?" Shelley asked.

"Of course I did," I said. "And she didn't do that much work."

"She's really stressed out. We talked about it the other day. You should support her."

"Yeah, well . . . it's hard doing a project alone," I said. "You wouldn't understand."

I was getting mad, and I couldn't say the reason. Shelley shouldn't really give *me* advice, you know? Advice was my job. Shelley should be giving support, which was what she had always done before.

There was this bluish green stone I liked, too.

Amazonite: *Helps calm the brain and nervous system.* I put that one in my pocket, too.

"You're only supposed to take one," Shelley whispered.

I shrugged.

Logan ran up to Shelley, hyped about something. "Colt just told me about equestrian summer camp. That is so cool!"

"Let's talk about that later, ya?" Shelley said.

"What are you talking about?" I asked.

"Shelley and Colt are going to equestrian camp!" Logan said.

Gives courage when needed most. Tigereye. I took that rock, too. I took three of them. I filled my pockets with crystals.

But none of them seemed to work.

Back in my life coaching training, I read that certain emotions can take over the decision-making process. Like for example, you could be a normally gracious and considerate person, but something or someone could push you over the edge and then you stop thinking clearly, filling up with a fiery furnace of ragey rage rage.

"STOP IT!" I shouted. "JUST STOP."

Shelley dropped the pink crystal she was holding. "Willis. Hey. Calm down."

"I am calm!" I shouted. "Everyone here is calm. It's like one big calm shower!"

Then Margo came from out of nowhere. Like, I'm

pretty sure she was inside eating organic honeycomb just a minute ago. She led me by the elbow. "Okay. Okay. Let's go somewhere else for a bit."

Logan tried to follow, but Shelley stopped her. "Give us a minute, K?"

Margo hurried us over to the side yard, which also had a spectacular view. How did this kid get this great of a party and this many pretty views?

"What is going on?" Margo asked. "We're all trying to decompress here. Now is not the time to start drama."

"I'm not." I pulled out a gold and brown crystal. I think it was the one that was supposed to help with courage. "Colt is."

"Colt?" Shelley looked around. "Colt's in the living room teaching breathing exercises. What does Colt have to do with this?"

I waved my hand in the air. "Everything! Colt has to do with everything!"

"Colt likes horses," Shelley said. "I like horses. What's the big deal?"

"And the soccer ball, Shells! Thanks for the get well card when my face got attacked by a soccer ball."

"My mom helped you right after you got hit," she said. "I didn't know you needed me to be a nurse, too."

"Not a nurse! A friend!"

Shelley turned to Margo. "Do you understand what he's flipping out over?"

Margo shook her head. "I'm . . . mostly I'm confused."

Now I turned on Margo. "What are you talking about, Spreadsheet? You totally agreed with me. Shelley leaves us all summer. Comes home and is this totally different person. She was a softball band girl, and now she's all horses, all the time. And Colt! She ditched us for Colt. That's why you made the plan for how we were going to win her back. Of course, you got so busy with your app, you forgot to follow through with it."

"You what?" Shelley's face reddened. "You guys are *spreadsheeting* me?"

"I . . . I . . . Well, you have been kinda gone," Margo said.

"I found my passion!" Shelley said. "What kind of friend gets mad at someone for finding their passion?"

"This isn't about your passion!" I pointed at Shelley. "You told me Colt is annoying, but still you're all 'yay crystals and horse camp'! It's not even October, and you're talking about summer *horse camp*?"

"I'm making plans!" Shelley said. "Which is better than what you did, sticking your whole passion project on Margo."

"Margo is my friend, and she totally wanted to help me, thanks."

"Um," Margo said. "Actually."

"And what did Colt ever do to you?" Shelley asked. "He's only ever been nice to you. He's tried talking to you, read your aura for free, offered to work with you, invited you to his house. You are so full of jealousy that you can't see that he's a nice kid. You're the bully."

The words hit me like a slap. Bully. Bully. *Bully*. I closed my eyes, grabbed one of the crystals in my pocket, and squeezed it super tight. I tried to breathe. I opened my eyes again.

Both of my friends were crying. Have you ever been so angry and looked at two faces of people you really care about and seen the most broken expressions? It will break your heart right into a million pieces.

Shelley didn't even say anything to me. She just marched around the corner.

Margo wasn't done. "My doctor said I have fatigue. Fatigue! I kept coming to you for advice or help—as a life coach or friend, I didn't care. But it was always just about you. You stopped listening. So you're fired as my life coach."

Then she stormed away, too, leaving me alone. I'd just broken every life coaching and friend rule in the book. I'd lost my cool at a social event. I'd stolen party favors. I'd hurt two of my best friends.

At least we were alone. I'd give us all a minute to simmer down, then I'd do damage control. I fixed my bow tie and walked around the side of the house. There were Logan, Spencer, Ella, Adrian. And great. Colt.

The awkward silence and stunned faces told me they'd all heard the whole thing.

PRO TIP #11:
Do not yell at clients and best friends during large social gatherings.

There was no coming back from something like this.

I didn't talk to anyone. I just ran out of that party and called my dad. When I got home, I hid under my blankets, where I planned to stay for the rest of my life.

CHAPTER 18

Everything Is Terrible!

The next day was Sunday, but I did not see the sun even once. I stayed in bed and told my mom to bring me all my meals there. The only meal I would have was chicken broth and Sprite. I didn't deserve solid food.

I was a mess. Everything was a mess. There was no way I could ever show my face again at school. I would have to call the doctor and tell them to put me on bedrest, which I think means I would never have to leave my bed again, except hopefully to use the bathroom. I would hang up my bow ties. My life of fancy was over.

At one point, Logan opened my door and set a plate of Dad's sugar cookies on the floor. But I didn't have the energy to walk across the room to eat them. And food sounded gross. And why had I said all those things to Shelley and would she ever talk to me again and why did the whole party have to hear and why did Colt move here and yes, I know this wasn't really his fault, but it made me feel a little better to feel bad about that, too.

Mom let me stay home Monday, even though she couldn't figure out what I was sick with.

That afternoon . . . at least, I think it was the afternoon—I'd lost all ability to count time—my door burst open, and all this light came in. Light is not your friend when you have cocooned yourself in darkness, so I rolled up into my blanket and waited for whatever human was standing there to leave.

"Willis. Get up."

I shielded my eyes against the brightness and saw

Margo at the foot of my bed. She had on her blue power suit, which looked especially powerful against my dingy gray sweats.

"No," I said. "I quit. Life coaching. Coaching. Life."

Margo patted my leg. "I know that was embarrassing. But I want you to know I forgive you."

"Thank you."

"Now, did you want to say something?" Margo asked.

Margo was acting super adulty right now. Annoyingly, as usual.

"Okay. I'm sorry. But you know . . . Shelley would have never found out about the spreadsheet if you hadn't made one in the first place."

"You really need to work on your apology skills. It's a good thing I'm so forgiving." Margo yanked the blanket off me. She had so much strength that she yanked me out of the bed with it. I hit the floor with a thud. "Willis, you are a stupendous life coach. You always know the right quote for the right situation. You give your clients space and time to figure out things. The only way you are going to get out of this . . . smelly mess is to start coaching again. I looked at your schedule. You have an appointment at six with Client A, whoever that is."

"But I still . . . um, I didn't input my app."

"I will help you for like ten minutes if you do your job right now," Margo said. "So get in the shower."

185

She didn't even wait for me to reply. She just slammed the door behind her. All business.

Dad was in the kitchen potting plants for Logan. Logan's entire passion project was spread across our kitchen table. She'd made take-home greenhouse kits so kids could have their own garden in any climate. She'd also grown six starter plants for each kit. She'd used most of her savings on gardening supplies. Logan planned ahead.

PRO TIP #12:
Spending most of your money on scented candles isn't smart financial planning.

Dad smiled when I came in, but it was one of those I-feel-sorry-for-you smiles. "Hey, there. You feeling better?"

"No."

"Logan told us what happened."

"Logan needs to finish her greenhouse kits and not

worry about my business," I said.

"She was pretty upset. Worried for you." Dad shoveled some soil into a pot. "She looks up to you, you know."

"Maybe she used to, but not anymore. Not after I've ruined everything."

Dad wiped his hands on his jeans and stared at me, like he didn't know what to do. I get this look from him a lot. I bet he did this the day I was born, like, who is this bawling baby, and what do I do with him?

Then he walked around the counter and swallowed me in a big hug. Hugging is usually Mom's territory, so this was super surprising. I patted his back awkwardly.

"You haven't ruined everything. You tried some things. Remember what Thomas Edison said about failure and results? Now you know several thousand things that won't work."

"Hey, I told you that quote," I said.

"You sure did. You're a great kid. Don't quit your

dream when you just started dreaming it."

You might think this is stupid, but my eyes got really wet all of a sudden. I hadn't cried at all that whole day, but there in the kitchen with my dad's shirt already wet from watering plants, I cried a whole bunch right into his sleeve.

Then I squared my shoulders and headed up to my closet. I had to pick the perfect outfit for my session with Adrian James.

CHAPTER 19

Adrian's Passion Project!

Adrian and I met at the basketball hoops at the park to do a practice run of his passion project. I set up a table and laid out a book with a rock on top to keep the pages open. There was also a comfy chair in case Adrian wanted to sit while he read and some ice water because sports and reading both demand that you stay hydrated.

Adrian stretched and shot a few basketballs. Yes, basketballs, plural! He had this basketball holder thing that let him shoot ball after ball. He grabbed a ball, the next one rolled forward. All very organized.

"You want to try, Will?" Adrian shot a ball in an arc. The net swooshed. "I teach you, you teach me. That kind of thing?"

"My face is still healing," I said.

"For real? It looks totally normal now."

"I don't want to get dirty," I said.

"You're wearing a tracksuit."

"Right." I fiddled with the zipper of my red jacket. "But it's a *brand-new* tracksuit. Come over here. We'll get started."

Obviously, I was a little sad that Adrian was an anonymous client, because I could have gotten so many sports clients from just this session! Kids would google something like "how to do a sports passion project with your life coach," and the video would pop right up! Then I would start getting Olympic athletes who would do their Olympic thing but also pursue other passions, too! Knitting and curling! Shot put and baking!

We'd do podcasts, TV shows, book deals—until we created a passion project amusement park, which would have sports AND science AND singing AND whatever. Since I invented the place, it would be called Willis World, and they would have Willis dolls and someone in a Willis costume walking around waving at kids and scaring them. And there would be bow ties and scarves in the gift shop. And my dad's sugar cookies. And—

"So I'm reading first?" Adrian asked.

Did you see that? My mind was full of ideas again. That was huge. I pulled out my stopwatch. "Yes, sirree! You'll read two pages out loud. Then you'll shoot ten baskets. I call the program READBOUND. Isn't that great? It's copyrighted, so no stealing." I clicked around on the stopwatch so I looked more official. "Your goal is to get as many pages and baskets as possible in ten minutes."

"Wait, I have to read *out loud*?" Adrian asked.

"Yeah, how else would we know if you're reading?"

Adrian looked like I just asked him to write a book. On the spot.

"Let's just try it, okay?" I said. "No pressure. It's just us."

Adrian opened to the first page of the book. It was a short book, one I read twice in second grade. He perched himself on the edge of the seat so he was all ready to go when the basketball part of my READBOUND program started.

"All right. Read!" I hit my stopwatch.

Adrian blinked at me for a few valuable seconds, then looked down at the page.

"There once . . . once . . . was a house . . . wait, no . . . a horse who everything . . . everyone knew had the . . . shinest . . . no that's not right . . . sheerest?"

"Shiniest," I said.

"Oh . . . shiniest hair." Adrian read for another five minutes. He didn't even finish the page.

"Great job!" I stopped the timer and handed him a basketball. "Maybe we'll just do one page at a time?"

"Look, Will, I would rather have a dentist come over and pull out all my teeth than read out loud like this. It's just so much pressure. Let's cut the reading part."

I stopped timing and leaned against the table. What to do? What to do? As a life coach, it wasn't my job to do things FOR the client. Like, I couldn't read the book for him. And if this wasn't his jam, it wasn't his jam. Everyone should have the jam they like. I'm a raspberry guy myself.

But I also knew that quitting things, especially important things, doesn't *fix* the thing. That was the hard lesson that I'd just learned—that I was still learning. It was the same with relationships. I couldn't let these friendships end because we'd hit a speed bump! I had to find a way to make things right. With Margo. With Shelley.

And okay. Yes. Colt.

Adrian grabbed the basketball from me and started shooting hoops. The first four went in. He made it look like the easiest thing in the galaxy.

"Okay, you ready for the next page?" I called.

"Nah." He shot another hoop. "Too bad you can't read for me."

"What do you mean?"

"Like, I understand it when I hear it. But when I'm looking at the words . . . it's jumbled."

And that's when I had a lightbulb idea!

So I once had this client who read every graphic novel she could get her hands on. There were stacks by her bed, under her bed. Sometimes she'd even start reading during a session! But her mom said graphic novels weren't "real books." Look, sometimes parents are just super wrong. So I looked into reading stuff, like what makes a book a book and what are the different kinds of reading. I found articles and everything. And one thing talked about auditory learners—people who learn best when they hear things instead of seeing them.

Solution: audiobooks!

"Adrian, what if someone could read for you?" I asked. "Well, not for you. But to you? Do you like audiobooks?"

Adrian dribbled the ball between his legs. "Yeah, we listen to those in class sometimes. I like when there's cool voices."

"Do you think you could listen and play basketball at the same time?"

"I'm listening to you now, right?" Adrian stepped back and shot the ball again. And it went in again. It was like magic.

Also magic: the revised READBOUND program. Adrian played basketball for another hour and listened to a book called *The Crossover* by Kwame Alexander, which he really liked. In fact, he told me he was going to stay and play so he could finish the book.

It was getting dark, so I packed up my little traveling office, ready to leave Adrian to his sports. TBH, I was still nervous with all those balls whooshing around within hitting distance of my face.

"Hey, Will." Adrian stopped dribbling his ball. "I'm really pumped now. Thanks."

That's when the *real* lightbulb moment hit me. Or maybe it was more of a lightning bolt?

Because this . . . this was what it was all about, wasn't it? Not about scholarships or trips to Washington, DC, podcasts or theme parks. It wasn't even about business cards or business competitions.

Life coaching was about *helping* people. I liked watching them grow and change. I liked being a part of it, but really . . . it wasn't about me at all. It didn't matter if anyone knew I coached Adrian. Adrian knew it, and Adrian mattered.

This process, these connections, this feeling . . . that was my real passion project.

CHAPTER 20

The Passion Fair!

How to Apologize and Move Forward

(From *Mental Light and Healing* magazine. This just showed up at my house one day. I suspected Colt.)

1. Recognize how you messed up.

2. Find an appropriate time and place to apologize.

3. Take responsibility.

4. Set boundaries.

5. Let go of your negative feelings (anger/jealousy/hurt).

6. Show love.

Principal Guinn had transformed the school into a learning wonderland. The projects were set up by grade and interest. If it involved a performance, those were played at set times in the theater. Some kids had videos playing on iPads if they'd prerecorded. Others had those big tri-fold cardboard posters from science fairs. The coolest part was how many kids participated. Classrooms were stuffed with creative ideas. The gym was totally full. Everyone and anyone would walk those halls tonight, witnessing all of Green Slope's passions.

I wore a hat because I didn't really want to show my face, which was still pretty swollen from all the good and bad crying I'd done. It was a fedora, because that's about the only hat that looks good with a bow tie.

My station was set up in the gym. I'd made a tri-fold poster with general information about life coaching. Behind me played the video interview I'd shot in the warehouse. I'd also made a poster explaining how to download the app.

I had a note saying that while I'd created the app content, Margo was the main designer. She deserved the credit. The template she gave me was extra easy to follow. I had my whole app live within two hours.

And it was amazing! Here's a screenshot of the main page:

The thing is, I didn't use technology that much. So even though I could give this to another kid to download, I didn't exactly know how to use it myself. After I'd launched it, Margo went in and added a few "bells and whistles," like a digital notebook to record thoughts. I asked why you wouldn't just use a notebook, because then you could buy a shiny notebook and write with a smooth gel pen. That frustrated her a little. I get it.

Margo's booth was right by mine. She actually had less stuff in her booth than me. Just a digital tablet that showed the app, a bowl of candy, and some balloons.

"Do you need help setting up the rest of your display?" I asked Margo.

"Nope. This is it."

I felt super guilty because it was obvious that she'd spread herself so thin working on my app that she hadn't finished her passion project.

"I'm sorry you didn't have more time to make this amazing."

Margo snorted. "Um, my app *is* amazing. It's because it's so amazing that I had no time to worry about the passion project part of this. Those investors bought shares of the app. We're taking it to beta school districts next week. They want to fly me out to Stanford for a college tech fair." She motioned toward the balloons. "I don't want to take this Passion Fair win away from someone else. That's why I dialed down my display. Which wasn't easy for me."

"Wow . . . that's huge. *Huge* news." I almost asked her why she didn't tell me, but we both knew the answer. I hadn't been a great friend or life coach lately. I'd apologized, but not very well, and now I would try harder. "I'm so proud of you. Margo, you are awesome."

She shrugged, but she was totally beaming. "I'll watch your booth if you want to walk around and check out the others. You still have a big chance to win this thing, you know. The app turned out great. You worked hard on that content."

"I won't win. Shelley and Colt are on the playground with a live horse right now." I tugged on my fedora. "You can't beat a horse."

"Well, you can land a lot of clients with this either way."

"You're right," I said. "The whole community was invited to this fair."

Margo smiled. "Finally. You're getting the big picture."

The whole fair was one really big picture! There were so many neat things! Huge murals and computers built from, I don't know, junk. Lego stop-motion movies and baking projects. Spencer and Ella built birdhouses for the elderly. They also gave out candy at their display, which had nothing to do with birds, but I still took a handful.

203

We had celebrities, too. Michael Morales, famous real estate agent, *waved at me*. Kelly Fordina, the anchorwoman on KRL, walked around interviewing students. Logan had a large crowd surrounding her greenhouse. She waved at me as I walked by. "Hey, brother, how is the app doing?"

"Margo said we got fifty downloads just today," I said. "The parents are going bananas for it."

"Cool! By the way, I did that thing you suggested. Life coaching plants. Look at the sign I made!" Logan pointed to a colorful display next to some of her plants: *Coach your plant to grow! Pick a positive affirmation and whisper away.*

I brought my hand to my chest. "I am . . . honored."

"Just don't ask for a commission when I go global with these greenhouse kits." Logan waved at a dad from our neighborhood. "Mr. Frotteur! Your tomato plants would do great using this new system . . ."

I circled around one more time. Talked to my parents. Circled. Visited Logan. Got some more candy from Ella and Spencer.

I was on my third circle when I literally bumped into Principal Guinn. She was dressed very professionally in a gray suit, but her rainbow braces were still *all* party.

"Willis! Oof." She steadied herself against the wall.

"Let's not give you another black eye, okay?"

"Dr. Guinn." I put on my bestest, most life-coachiest smile. "Congratulations! This is spectacular."

She surveyed the gym. "It really is, isn't it? Just wait and see what I have planned for reading week."

"Well, I better head back to my display."

"Which was stupendous!" She gave me an actual thumbs-up. "You should be really proud of your hard work. And wow—I just talked to Adrian James. What a creative project. He told me that you life-coached him through some difficult things."

"Adrian? Adrian told you . . . about me? Coaching?"

She jutted her thumb toward the playground. "Well, yes. It's part of his presentation. Didn't you see it?"

"Um, no." I crossed and uncrossed my arms. "I, uh, haven't made it to the outdoor displays yet."

Dr. Guinn checked her watch. "You better hurry! We are announcing the winner in fifteen minutes. And

206

your friend is out there. Mrs. Kalani's daughter."

"Shelley. Yeah."

Maybe you can't tell because I'm so good at staying professional and hiding my feelings, but . . . I'd been avoiding going outside all night. Even though I'd read that article about apologizing and even though I was ready to do it . . . I was also nervous. There was a chance they wouldn't forgive me, or even talk to me.

Going outside would take a lot of gumption, and I was worried I'd used up all of that.

But I also remembered a quote that I'd been trying not to remember all night.

"Mistakes are always forgivable if one has the courage to admit them"—Bruce Lee.

So I said a professional goodbye to Dr. Guinn and pushed through the gym doors to the playground outside.

CHAPTER 21

Everyone's a Winner!

Adrian's display was the first one outside. He had a Little Tykes basketball hoop set up for kids and audiobooks playing in the background. A large purple sign shouted READBOUND! There was even a picture of me next to his explanation of the program.

"Will! My man!" Adrian gave me one of those fist-bump/hand-shake/high-five combos that I always got wrong but felt so cool doing. "I checked out your app earlier. Solid work."

"Yeah, hey. Adrian. This is . . . You did it. Like, all

the way. For real." My eyes were wide and maybe a little wet. Is this how teachers or parents feel? This pride that someone they care about has done such an awesome thing?

"I gave you a shout-out, too." He motioned to my picture. My school picture from last year, which wasn't my best, but still a nice gesture. "Everyone's asking about your life coaching. Margo said other kids have mentioned it at your booth."

"Why?" I asked simply. "Why would you tell people? I thought you didn't want anyone to know."

He rubbed the back of his neck. "Yeah. I don't know. I was at Colt's party."

"And you heard me get in a fight," I said. Oh great, he pitied me.

"No, um. He had these crystals? And there was this purple one, charoite or something, that said it could help with transforming and overcoming fear. Which I totally needed to do. To own my stuff and be cool with it, you know?"

"So a rock made you do it." Look, I'm sure crystals have excellent healing powers, but it still stung that a card at Colt's party brought this awakening instead of, I don't know, nine life coaching sessions.

"Nah. You did," Adrian said. "You've been great all summer, dude. And I wanted other people to know about it. So I finally started speaking up."

Adrian grabbed the mini basketball and banked another shot. A whole bunch of kids circled around him, wanting to chat. People always wanted to be around Adrian James, VIP.

But even VIPs got scared or insecure. They needed help sometimes. We all did.

Adrian's acknowledgment gave me the final drop of courage to face Shelley. There was a line snaking around her booth. Colt's mom had parents filling out forms in order to see the horse. Because yeah, they had a horse! Spices, the horse I'd groomed at the stable. Shelley was by her side, petting her nose. The smile on Shelley's face was electric. It was the smile of someone who was living their passion.

The smile slipped for a second when she saw me. I gave a little wave. She whispered something to Colt, who looked up at me. He didn't smile or frown, just nodded. Shelley weaved around the kids and met me on the blacktop, right on the four-square court, where we'd played together countless times.

"I didn't think you'd come out here," she said.

"Me neither." I let out a shaky breath. "I'm sorry."

"Me too."

"What for?"

She looked up. "I should have done something nice when you hurt your face. I think I was still mad about you being bossy about the passion project, and . . . things

211

have just been weird, right?"

"Yeah. My fault. I got so jealous. And scared that I would lose you."

"Never."

"Ever?" I asked.

"Our interests are going to change," she said. "But we will always be friends."

And then Shelley hugged me. She smelled like horses. Not bad-smelling horses. Just hay. And friendship.

Dr. Guinn's voice came through the speaker. "Thank you, everyone—students, parents, members of the community—for attending our Passion Fair today. The PTO did an excellent job putting this together, and we raised over one thousand dollars to go toward our arts program! You can all cheer."

People started clapping and hollering. Community is so cool!

"I'm going to announce our winners now. Afterward, I will meet them in their booths with a camera crew."

"I better get back," Shelley said.

"Yeah. Me too. Tell Colt . . . Tell him I'd like to talk to him later."

I bolted back to the booth. Adrian was right—there were lots of kids by my booth, more than even earlier that night. When Margo saw me, she grabbed my hand. "This is it!"

Dr. Guinn stood on the stage with a microphone.

213

"First I want to say, everyone tonight is a winner," she said. "You found something that interested you and went after it. I know a lot of adults who live their whole lives without pursuing their passion. So snaps for all."

More cheering and self-congratulating. I stayed frozen.

"We have two winners and two honorable mentions." Dr. Guinn continued. "There's a winner for grades one through three and a winner for grades four and five. These winners and their families will accompany me to the National Passion Fair in DC this spring. The honorable mentions get a little surprise and a nice certificate. So without further ado . . . our one through three honorable mention is Maisie McMann and Gavin Zhao for their Sugar Versus Honey project. Our four and five honorable mention is Colt Whiting and Shelley Kalani for their Equine Therapy project!"

Suddenly my feet were off the floor. I was jumping

and dancing and so, so happy for Shelley. Margo was squealing and fist pumping, too, in a very unprofessional but PERFECT way. I couldn't wait to run outside and congratulate their faces off.

"And our winners are . . . for grades one through three, Logan Wilbur and Abby Tam for their Greenhouse Kits. For grades four and five, David Weizel and Natalia Duval for their Lego Robot project."

My stomach dropped and then jumped and then shimmied around. I didn't hear my name. I didn't win.

But my sister did!

"I'll go see Shelley." Margo pushed me toward the door. "You see Logan first."

I sprinted down the hallway and to Logan's booth in a back classroom. The camera crew was already in there, same as my parents, who had their arms around Logan as she chattered to the interviewer. I ran right into the shot and gave her a hug. "You did it!"

Logan didn't even skip a beat. She scooted me right next to her and fixed my bow tie into place. Her made-for-TV smile stayed on the whole time.

"And this is my brother and former employer, Willis," Logan said. "Check out his life coaching app! But only after you purchase one of my at-home greenhouse kits."

This wasn't the way I thought things would go. But when does that ever happen, anyway?

I stood next to my little sister, grinning at the camera, squeezing my mom's hand. What a ride. I was going to Washington, DC, with my family to cheer on my genius sister.

And huh, while I was there, it wouldn't hurt to offer my life coaching services to kids of politicians. Do some group sessions. Mix and mingle at a few galas. Maybe even begin my own political campaign.

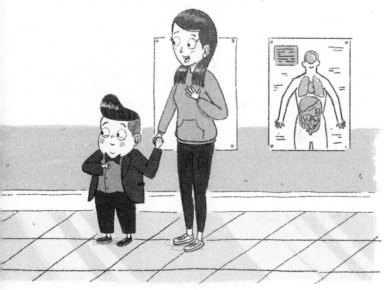

President Wilbur sounds fantastic, right?

Once the photos were taken, I ran outside to find Shelley. But she had so many people around her, it was impossible to get in. Which was okay. We were okay. We would celebrate later.

Colt, however, was alone with the horse. I knew it was the right time and the right place.

"Hey, Colt." I smiled. "Congrats on your big win."

"Thanks. It was a great experience."

"So." I reached into my pocket and pulled out a handful of crystals. The handful of crystals I'd accidentally stolen at his party. "I took these. I'm sorry."

"I guess they called to you. Keep them. Although I wouldn't put that tigereye by an amazonite. Amazonite helps you sleep, while tigereye keeps you up. Bad combo."

"Oh yeah. Okay." I put the green one on the table next to Colt. I really wanted to keep the tigereye. "That's not the thing I really wanted to apologize for, though.

218

I was . . . Look, I never really gave you a chance. I saw you as a threat even though you were nice to me. It wasn't fair. And I'm sorry."

Colt cracked a smile. "That was a fantastic apology. Did you have that ready before?"

"Well, yeah. I read some articles."

"Okay, cool."

"Cool?" I would not have let Colt off so easy. But that's what Colt was—easy. I could use some of his laid-back nature.

"Absolutely. And now that we're friends, there's something I want to run by you."

I hadn't exactly said we were *friends* yet, but if he was feeling positive, I should, too. "What's that?"

"What if we opened an office together?"

My mouth did not move. Neither did my brain.

"We're both coaches, but totally different kinds. We actually aren't competing, just offering different services to different people. Some kids might need you. Some kids might need me. Some kids might need us both."

"So . . . it would grow our client list and help us reach a wider audience?"

Colt snapped his fingers. "Bingo."

Even though this idea was out of the blue, like so out of the *ocean* blue, it still had a lot of potential. I could rent my office space to Colt when I wasn't meeting with clients. Later, we could knock out a wall to expand the business. Probably buy the house from my parents so we'd have space while we built our own office/warehouse. You know what else? Podcasts sound so much better when there are two people talking together. So do morning talk shows. And wow, I could really help him out with some things—calling people colors, wearing more professional attire. I guess he could teach me some things, too. What he'd said to me in the hallway that one time made a lot of sense.

PRO TIP #13:
Even life coaches need coaches.

"Let's schedule a brunch to discuss the possibilities," I said. "But I do have one condition."

"What's that?"

"You need to re-read my aura," I said.

Colt looked me up and down. I made sure to think azure blue thoughts.

"You're right. I'm getting some other colors."

"What are they?" I asked excitedly.

"I'll tell you once we're partners."

Huh. Wilbur & Whiting Life Coaching has a good ring to it, right?

THE END

Photo © Erin Summerill

Lindsey Leavitt is the author of over fifteen books for kids, tweens, and teens. She once ran on a gym treadmill next to the actor Nicolas Cage, but he was faster, so now she runs outside. Hahaha, okay, she doesn't run so much as stroll. Most of those strolls are between her office and her kitchen. Lindsey has an MFA from Vermont College of Fine Arts. Visit her website at www.lindseyleavitt.com.